*The Doomsday Marshal
and the Hanging Judge*

Also by Ray Hogan

OUTLAW'S EMPIRE
THE RAWHIDERS
THE DOOMSDAY CANYON
THE VENGEANCE OF FORTUNA WEST
THE RENEGADE GUN
THE DOOMSDAY BULLET
LAWMAN'S CHOICE

The Doomsday Marshal and the Hanging Judge

and RAY HOGAN

DOUBLEDAY & COMPANY, INC.
GARDEN CITY, NEW YORK
1987

All of the characters in this book
are fictitious, and any resemblance
to actual persons, living or dead,
is purely coincidental.

Library of Congress Cataloging-in-Publication Data

Hogan, Ray, 1908–
    The doomsday marshal and the hanging judge.

        I. Title.
PS3558.03473D635 1987   813'.54   86-16557
        ISBN 0-385-23562-3

For
My sister Eleanor Hogan Hackett,
her Frank and their legacies:
Herb, Trudy, June and Jim . . .

The Doomsday Marshal and the Hanging Judge

"Ain't a jail in this whole damn two-bit territory that can hold me," Milo Dodge said.

John Rye, pulling to a halt on a rise overlooking Arizona's capital city of Prescott, slid a sardonic glance at the outlaw.

"Seems that jail tree in Wickenburg did a good job of keeping you tied down."

Dodge shrugged. Raising his manacled hands, he brushed at his full dark beard. A heavyset, powerful man with small black eyes peering out from beneath heavy brows, he was a pitiless killer who gloried in the number of lives he had taken—nine in all. He viewed the law and all lawmen with scorn and had made good so far his continual boast of escaping the punishment due him.

"Fact is we ain't reached the calaboose yet. There's a couple of miles yet till we get to that town."

Rye, famed as the Doomsday Marshal, efficient and utterly ruthless when it came to handling outlaws, continued to coolly consider Dodge. A hard smile parted his lips.

"Go ahead," he drawled, untying the lead rope attached to the outlaw's horse and letting it fall free, "do me and the country a favor: make a run for it."

Dodge frowned angrily as he watched Rye's hand drop to the butt of the hair-trigger .45 Colt he carried on his hip.

"You saying I'd be scared to try?" he asked in a none too firm voice.

The lawman smiled again. "I figure you're damn fool enough to try anything—'specially since you'll be swinging at the end of a rope before the month's over."

"Don't take no bets on it," Dodge grumbled and turned away.

Rye laughed, took up the rope to the outlaw's horse, secured it once again to a ring on his saddle skirt. "Move out," he said, and when Dodge started forward he raked the chestnut he was riding lightly with his spurs and sent him moving down the trail for the settlement also.

He'd be damn glad when he got Milo Dodge off his hands. The outlaw had been trouble ever since he'd taken charge of the man at Wickenburg, where the town marshal had also been more than happy to rid himself of the outlaw. Rye had just finished delivering a prisoner to the prison at Yuma when he received word from headquarters to swing by the mining town of Wickenburg, pick up Milo Dodge and escort him to Prescott.

Dodge, chained to a large mesquite tree near the center of the town, since the settlement had no jail, put up a fight from the start, forcing Rye to knock him unconscious with a blow from the sawed-off shotgun he carried on his saddle. Such positive treatment had served to settle the outlaw down for the first three days of the five-day journey, but as they had drawn nearer their destination Dodge had become more difficult, causing innumerable problems and delays designed to slow their progress.

Rye took it all in stride. During his years as a special

U.S. marshal with far-ranging privileges, he had contended with a good number of outlaws with Milo Dodge's turn of mind and thus was unaffected by the man's obvious attempts to create a distraction that would enable him to escape. No prisoner had ever succeeded in getting away from John Rye, whose creed appeared to be that he would deliver his charge to the designated point either dead or alive; it all depended upon the wishes of the prisoner.

Rye looked ahead at Dodge. The outlaw was slouched in his saddle, eyes fixed on his hands resting on the horn. It would seem Dodge had given up any thought of trying to make a break, evidently deciding to wait and take his chances after he reached Prescott. The marshal shook his head at the thought; the town had a pretty good jail, one that was about as escapeproof as could be made. If Milo Dodge broke out of it he would accomplish a feat no other prisoner had ever done.

Rye raised his glance to the lower part of the wooded trail, and beyond to the town itself. Prescott, lying quiet along the stream called Granite Creek, seemed deserted in the warm summer sunlight. But the settlement would be far from that stage, Rye knew; it was simply the noon hour and people were inside their homes or in the restaurants and like places where meals could be obtained, having their lunch.

He could see a number of horses in a corral at the south end of town; several wagons and buggies were pulled up along the main street while off to the north a lone cowboy was driving a small jag of cattle along the north road that led to Fort Whipple. Prescott was very much alive but at that hour the hot Arizona sun and hunger were having their way.

Abruptly a deer bolted across the trail in front of Dodge. The horse the outlaw was riding shied violently, reared and spilled him from the saddle. Immediately the outlaw seized the opportunity to make his break. Dodging to one side, he ducked into the brush, struggling all the while to throw off the rope that encircled his waist while his riderless horse galloped on down the long slope.

Dodge had misjudged John Rye. The lawman had not used the usual sliding knot in the rope when he placed it about the outlaw; he had used instead the old reliable square or reef knot. Jerk and twist as he did while plunging off through the trees and brush, Dodge could not free himself from the rope.

Rye, still in the saddle and following along at a pace that kept the lariat fairly taut, allowed the outlaw to make his way to the bottom of the slope. Reaching there, he drew the chestnut to a quick halt—so abruptly in fact that it jerked the outlaw off his feet and sent him sprawling into the dust and dry leaves.

Cursing raggedly, sucking hard for breath, Dodge rolled over and glanced up at Rye, his eyes glowing with hate. The packhorse, trained to follow the chestnut, halted behind the big gelding and began to nibble at the short grass along the edge of the trail.

"Enjoy your run?" Rye asked dryly.

"Go to hell!" Dodge shot back angrily and got to his feet. "Why didn't you use your gun on me?"

"Too easy—for you. I'm saving you for hanging."

Another burst of oaths poured from the outlaw's flaring mouth. He was still breathing heavily.

"Would've been doing me a favor . . . Where's my horse?"

Rye gestured toward town with a thumb. "He kept on going. Means you'll be walking the rest of the way."

"The hell! I ain't going to take one step—"

"Suit yourself," Rye said and, clucking to the chestnut, moved out ahead of the outlaw.

The rope around Milo Dodge tightened. He rocked forward as the chestnut began a steady walk across the flat lying between the hill and the town. Dodge, stumbling into a trot, began a fresh round of cursing as he struggled to retain his footing. Rye, unmoved, glanced back. The outlaw fell again, managed to pull himself upright again and continue on, stumbling, reeling from side to side, going to his knees and righting himself again and again.

Persons began to appear along the street as Rye and his prisoner entered, some coming out of doorways, some from the passageways between the buildings, while others crowded up to both the lower and the upper windows of the buildings. Rye seemed not to notice but rode on, eyes straight ahead, relentlessly dragging Milo Dodge down the town's main street to the sheriff's office.

Reaching there the marshal headed the chestnut into the hitch rack and taking the lariat in his hands drew the swearing, cursing, dust-covered outlaw in close. As he dismounted a young deputy stepped out onto the board landing that fronted the combination office and jail.

"Howdy, Mr. Rye," he said. "You remember me? I'm Charley Hoskins." He turned his attention then to the dozen or so onlookers who had quickly gathered and shook his head in warning. Then, "You brought in Dodge, I see."

Rye, walking up to the outlaw, removed the rope

from around his waist and the manacles that linked his wrists together.

"Yeh, I remember you, Deputy," and then nodded at the outlaw. "He's a mite messed up. Decided to walk the last mile."

"Dragged you mean," a voice coming from among the crowd commented. "You're pretty hard on a man, ain't you, Marshal?"

Rye ignored the question. Accustomed to such observations from civilians who, naturally, were always totally ignorant of what had transpired on an occasion such as this, he had long ago elected to remain silent and ignore unwarranted remarks. The good people of the land, on the whole, were a strange lot: they wanted law and order but when it became necessary for a lawman to handle a criminal in the manner he deserved, the bleeding hearts complained to high heaven.

"Jones— The sheriff around?" Rye asked, prodding Dodge toward the door of the jail with his gun.

"Nope, had to go to Tucson. Left me in charge."

"I see. Well, open up your best cell and I'll stash this jasper in it. Want you to lock it good and then make sure you hide the key. He'll get away from you if you give him half a chance; fact is he just the same as promised he would."

"The hell he will!" the deputy said. "We've collared worse than him and they never got away."

"Well, keep a close watch on him," Rye said, shoving the outlaw into the iron cage. "He's busted out of several other places."

"He sure won't here," the deputy declared, locking the door of the cell, and turned back into the office area. "Got a letter for you, Marshal. Come a couple of days ago. It's from Washington."

Rye swore softly. A letter from headquarters could mean only one thing: another hurry-up assignment such as the one he had just completed. He had looked forward to lying around Prescott for a few days, resting up, chewing the rag with Sheriff Abe Jones, but if things ran according to the usual pattern, he'd likely be on the trail again by the next day.

2

Deputy Charley Hoskins crossed to the cluttered rolltop desk in the back of the room and drew an envelope from one of the pigeonholes. Handing it to the lawman he said: "Sheriff told me to be sure and give it to you if you showed up while he was gone. Figured, coming from Washington, it'd be mighty important."

Rye took the brown envelope from the deputy, slit it open with the knife he carried inside his shield-type shirt, and unfolded the letter. It was from the chief U.S. marshal, the man to whom he was directly responsible. As he read the brief message, he frowned irritably.

"Something wrong?" Hoskins asked, watching the lawman closely.

Rye shook his head. "No, I reckon you couldn't say there's anything wrong—just a job I sure won't be looking forward to."

Hoskins rubbed at his jaw, glanced out into the street. Two riders had pulled up at the hitch rack of the Goldminer's Saloon and were dismounting hurriedly. About twenty years of age, tall, lean, straw-haired, ruddy-faced, he had the eager look of youth about him. Charley would probably make a good lawman, Rye had thought upon first meeting him, if he learned to bridle his impatience and didn't get too anxious to make a name for himself.

"Expect you ain't got much choice other'n to do what you're told—being the kind of marshal you are."

"Never turned down a job yet," Rye said, folding the letter and thrusting it into a pocket. "There's been a few I didn't like, but the job had to be done."

"Seems I recollect you being a Special U.S. Marshal for a long time," Hoskins said when it became apparent Rye wasn't going to discuss the orders he'd received from Washington. "I think I heard the sheriff say you was appointed by President Hayes. Sure must've made you proud having the President do the appointing."

"Any man wearing a star has the right to be proud, no matter who pinned it on him . . . How far is Clear Springs from here, and which direction?"

"The Springs? Maybe a day's ride due west. It's along the Verde River. Just follow the road. That where you're going next?"

"The way it looks—"

"Mind telling me what for? Don't aim to be nosy but the sheriff'll want to know all about everything—and Clear Springs is in our county."

Rye's shoulders stirred indifferently. "Being sent there to escort a fellow—a judge—to his home in Nebraska. Seems he's quitting, but he's made a lot of enemies around the country and I've been handed the job of seeing he gets back home alive."

Hoskins had drawn a sack of Bull Durham from his shirt pocket and was expertly rolling himself a cigarette.

"This here judge you're talking about; his name wouldn't be Metzgar, would it—Asa Metzgar?"

Rye nodded, a tight smile on his long lips. "Yeh, it would—the one they call the Hanging Judge."

The deputy whistled softly, finished making his smoke, and hung the slim cylinder in the corner of his mouth. "So that's what happened to him. He just sort of disappeared not long after the Dixon hanging. Well, I sure ain't hankering for your job! That man's got more yahoos looking to put a bullet in him than a steer's got ticks. You know him?"

Rye grinned at the exaggeration but he guessed Asa Metzgar did have more enemies than any man should have.

"Yeh, I know him—from over Texas way—New Mexico, too. He was one that sort of kept on the move."

"That ain't hard to savvy. The way he run his court and handed out hangings, it probably wasn't healthy for him to stay in one place more'n a year or so."

Rye got to his feet, sauntered to the doorway and had his look at the street. The crowd that had gathered when he rode in with Milo Dodge at the end of his rope had disappeared, and Prescott had now returned to its normal daily routine.

He was wishing the Chief Marshal had picked someone else to escort Metzgar to his home, but he hadn't and there was nothing to be done about it. Rye didn't particularly like Asa Metzgar—not that he held it against the jurist for his harshness in dealing with outlaws; any man who killed or otherwise broke the law deserved what he got; it was just the fact that Metzgar seemed to take pleasure in executing the men found guilty by him or a jury to the point of making a spectacle of the incident—such as hanging four or five men at a time.

Perhaps such exhibitions were good for the country, as Asa Metzgar had once claimed—saying that such grisly exhibitions put the fear of God in would-be law-breakers as well as hardened outlaws—but Rye saw a certain ghoulishness in it. And for a lawman known to have little compassion for the criminals he was sent to deal with, that was a paradox.

"Metzgar make any enemies around here?" he asked, turning back to the deputy.

Hoskins, not bothering to remove the cigarette from the corner of his mouth, nodded. "Sure did. Several, but I reckon the ones that hate his guts the most are the Dixons. They've got a farm, or maybe it ought to be called a ranch, north of here about twenty miles in the Chino Valley country. The judge hung two of the boys."

"They try putting a bullet in the judge?"

"Couple of shots were taken at him that come mighty close. That's when he picked up and left. Nobody knew where he'd gone—and we hadn't heard nothing about him quitting being a judge and high-tailing it for home." The deputy paused, flipped the butt of his cigarette into a bucket of sand set near the doorway and added: "Sheriff's going to take it real hard that he wasn't picked to take the judge to wherever he's going. It'll hurt his feelings some."

"Be glad to turn the job over to him if I could," Rye said. "Any of the Dixons hanging around now?"

"Seen Gar—he's the old man—about a week ago at Kaseman's Saloon. Devon, the only son the judge didn't hang, ain't been around in some time."

"Big family?"

"Only Gar and Devon are left. And I reckon you best figure in Saul Hillman, too. He's Gar's brother-in-law. They've been thicker'n thieves ever since the judge hung Price and Cord."

"They have it coming?"

Hoskins shrugged. "I reckon they did. They was seen out at the Caffrey place one afternoon by a couple of cowhands. Later old man Caffrey run into them leaving his ranch. They sort of dodged him, he said when he was telling the judge about it, but there weren't no doubt who they were and where they'd been."

"When he got to his place his wife was dead along with both the daughters. They was about sixteen—and twins. The woman had been hit over the head with something, and the girls"—Hoskins paused, shook his head—"you can about figure what them hellions done to them. They were right pretty, too."

"Metzgar hang the Dixons?"

"Yeh, but not here. Was at a town on west. Feeling was running mighty high and the sheriff didn't want nobody interfering. He swore in a half dozen special deputies and moved the Dixons out one midnight. They strung them up early that next morning."

"The Dixon boys ever admit they'd killed the two girls and their mother?"

"No, claimed all along they didn't—even tried to say they never been on the Caffrey place, but they was lying through their teeth when they said that. Them cowhands seen them, and old man Caffrey sure wasn't lying.

"Of course there was a few folks who didn't think the Dixons had done it. There was bad blood between the two families—the Dixons and the Caffreys—and some figured the Caffreys blamed what somebody else had done on the Dixons."

"Just taking advantage of the situation—"

"Yeh, that's it, but the judge didn't cotton to that

kind of thinking—and neither did the sheriff. Them two Dixon boys was bad clean through, and far as I'm concerned they got exactly what was coming to them."

Rye got to his feet. Reaching into an inside pocket he procured a nearly flat leather case, opened it, offered one of the long slim stogies it contained to the deputy. Hoskins declined with a shake of his head and drew out his sack of makings and prepared to roll himself another cigarette.

Selecting one of the cigars, Rye bit off its closed end, spat the bit of tobacco into the bucket of sand that served as a cuspidor and struck a match with his thumbnail. Holding the flame to the end of the stogie, he slowly sucked it into life, exhaled a cloud of smoke and leaned against the wall. Sweat lay on his rugged, square face in thin patches, and taking off his flat-crowned hat he ran long fingers through his dark hair.

"Got to depend on you not mentioning where I'm headed—not to anybody," he said.

"Not even to the sheriff?"

"When'll he be back?"

"Tomorrow night, I figure—"

"Go ahead, tell him. I'll be gone by then. Just that I don't want anybody to know where I'm headed—and why."

"'Cepting him—"

"Yeh, he'll understand why I need to keep everything quiet . . . What do these Dixons look like?"

"Gar, the old man, is about forty-five, sort of heavy-set, got real sharp blue eyes and a round face. Hair's dark. He's mean and tough; can easy spot him by the big Texas-style black hat he'll be wearing.

"Devon, he's the son, is about twenty-five now and

looks a lot like his pa. Ain't ever seen him when he don't have a rifle in the crook of his arm. Saul Hillman's a real tall fellow with a sharp face; makes a man think of a hawk when he looks at him. Always wears regular old sodbuster overalls and shoes. He lives with the Dixons, being Mattie Dixon's brother."

"They're hard cases, all three of them. I reckon you could say Price and Cord come by their cussedness naturally."

Rye was silent for a time as he digested the information and then, resetting his hat, nodded to the deputy.

"Obliged to you, Hoskins. Like I said, keep what I'm here to do to yourself. I brought in Milo Dodge and that's all anybody, other'n you and the sheriff, needs to know."

"Yes, sir," the deputy said. "Anything more I can do for you?"

"Nope, you've done plenty. Aim to stable my horses now, clean up, eat, get a good night's sleep and then head for this Clear Springs first thing in the morning . . . If you spot a stray horse around somewhere close it'll belong to Dodge. Can do what you want with it . . . Livery stable's on down the street a piece, I recollect."

"Maybe a hundred yards, on your right. You know where the hotel is."

Rye nodded and stepped out into the street. A few persons were to be seen going about their various duties now that the noon hour and the excitement was over, and crossing to the chestnut gelding the lawman freed the reins and swung up into the saddle. Cutting away from the hitch rack, and with the bay packhorse following along, he headed for the livery barn.

3

"Gabe's Livery Stable," the gold-and-red sign on the front of the building declared. Squat and broad, its corrugated tin roof shining in the sunlight, it was set back a few yards from the street. In deference to the summer heat its wide front door was open.

Rye rode the chestnut into the structure's runway and drew to a halt. A few moments later a man in stained undershirt and overalls, shoes caked with dung and mud, strolled into view from the rear of the shadow-filled building.

"Howdy," he greeted, shifting his cud of tobacco from one cheek to the other as the lawman stepped down. "Sure is a mighty fine-looking horse you got there."

Rye nodded in agreement. "Needs looking after. Want him rubbed down, watered and grained. Same for the pack horse. You the one that'll be doing it?"

"Reckon I am because Gabe ain't around. My name's Ollie. You putting up for the night or you just stopping by?"

"Be for the night most likely—but when you're done with them stable them in stalls where they'll be handy. Might have to leave early."

"Won't be nobody here after midnight to saddle up for you," Ollie warned.

"Can manage that myself. How much?"

"Going to be a dollar apiece."

Rye reached into his pocket, produced the two specified coins along with one additional. "The extra dollar's for you so's you'll see that my horses are taken care of right."

The hostler's stubble-covered face brightened at once. "Sure—I sure will, mister. Can figure on me."

"I'll be over at the Dawson Hotel," Rye said, and took his saddlebags and shotgun off the chestnut. "Can find me there if you want me. Where'll my horses be?"

"Right there in them two front stalls. They'll be real handy, just like you want . . . Say, wasn't that you I seen bringing a prisoner into the sheriff's office a bit ago?"

"It was. Killer named Milo Dodge," the marshal said and turned toward the door.

Ollie whistled softly. "Jeez! Was that Dodge? What are you, some kind of a lawman or a boun—"

The hostler's voice faltered at the term. Rye's lips pulled down into a half smile. "No, I'm no bounty hunter," he said, and letting the subject drop there, crossed the dusty street to the hotel.

The clerk, a small, thin man wearing, among other necessary clothing, a high celluloid collar that appeared to be choking him, pushed the dog-eared register toward Rye. The inside of the hotel had recently had a coat of paint and the smell was still in the air.

"One night or more?" he asked, squinting through thick-lensed pince-nez glasses as he handed a pencil to Rye.

"One," the lawman said, signing the book.

"Be a dollar and a half—in advance."

Rye forked over the necessary amount, reached for the key the hotel man had taken from a hook on a board behind him and turned to the narrow hallway leading off what served as a lobby.

"You didn't put down where you come from," the clerk called, halting him. "Law says you got to write that down same as you do your name."

"Yuma," Rye said. "You write it down."

Continuing on, the lawman made his way along the stuffy corridor to room 5. The door was unlocked; he entered and laid the shotgun and saddlebags across the bed. Crossing immediately to the lone window, he raised it, allowing the trapped heat to escape and admitting a measure of fresh air. At that moment a step sounded at the door. It was the clerk.

"Bringing you a pitcher of water and a clean towel in case you want to wash up," he said.

"Thanks. I appreciate that," the lawman said.

He'd gone through the procedure of entering a strange town, stabling his horse (or horses, depending on the situation) and signing in for a hotel room more times than he cared to count, Rye thought, but this room, despite its faded carpet, garish wallpaper and scarred furniture, appeared much cleaner than the average.

"Where can a man get a good meal around here?" he asked as the clerk turned to go.

"Half Moon Restaurant on the corner. A Chinee runs it," the hotel man replied. "Kelly's Saloon puts out a good meal, too—if you don't mind the drunks."

"Never like to mix my eating with my drinking," Rye said. "One spoils the other."

"Sure does," the clerk said and hurried out of the room.

Following the man to the door Rye closed and locked it, after which he stripped and washed himself down from the china bowl and the pitcher of water. Drying off, he drew on the same clothing he had removed, strapped on his gun and returned to the street.

The heat had softened considerably compared to what it had been when he rode into the settlement, and moving on down the board sidewalk he located the Half Moon Restaurant and entered, selecting for himself a table near the back of the fairly large room. He had barely settled onto his chair when a young Chinese girl hurried up with a glass of water.

"You want steak and potato?" she asked in a high, almost childish voice.

"They'll do fine," the lawman said. "Want coffee too."

The girl bowed and hurried away to repeat the order in a singsong voice to someone behind a partition covered with paper cutouts of scenes from various magazines.

Rye shifted his attention to the street, visible through several medium-sized windows. The glass was clean and it was pleasing to note the absence of dead flies on the sills.

A good, well-cooked meal would taste good, the lawman thought, idly watching a man and a woman in a red-wheeled buggy pass by. He had been fixing his grub on the trail since leaving Yuma, except for the brief stopover in Wickenburg, and while years on the move in the pursuit of his profession had made him a good trail cook, supper in a restaurant would be a treat.

The food came quickly, well prepared and tasty. The cook had fried the steak with no additional garnishments other than salt, which was just the way Rye liked it; the potatoes were crisp and brown while the biscuits, buttered and topped with honey, were light and flaky. The side portion of tender beans was just enough, and the coffee, while a trifle weak in comparison to his usual camp brew, was good.

When he had finished Rye got to his feet. Immediately the girl hurried up. "Is it all right?" she asked anxiously.

He nodded. "Supper was fine. I was a mite hungry, I reckon. Made me eat in a hurry."

He paid the charge she quoted and leaving the Half Moon went back onto the street. Prescott had become somewhat busier than when he had first arrived, there now being several wagons and buggies pulled up along the street while two dozen or more persons, including a few uniformed soldiers, were moving about.

Taking his leisure along the sidewalk, the lawman made his way to the livery stable, intending to look in on his horses, see if they were being cared for properly. After that he'd drop by the jail, chew the cud with deputy Charley Hoskins for a bit.

Reaching the livery barn, he glanced in, saw the hostler busy at rubbing down the chestnut. Both animals had been stripped of their gear and were feeding from the manger at the end of their stalls. Ollie was giving the horses his best.

Satisfied, Rye turned away and started for the jail. Deputy Hoskins had just come out of the sheriff's office, was cutting hurriedly across the street and heading for a destination at the far end of town. With time heavy on his hands, as was always the way when he was not actively engaged, Rye stepped to the inside of the walk and, leaning back to the wall of the building, moodily considered the street.

Kelly's Saloon . . . The marshal's eyes paused on its ornate batwing doors directly opposite. A shot of good whiskey would hit the spot—actually top off the fine meal he'd enjoyed at the Half Moon. And, too, it might perhaps ease the slight tension the letter from Washington had created.

The saloon had no more than a half dozen patrons at that early-evening hour, and entering the dimly lit building, its walls decorated with glassy-eyed deer heads, pictures from calendars, the yellowed front page of an Eastern newspaper detailing the assassination of Abraham Lincoln, and various other articles that had taken the owner's fancy, Rye stepped up to the counter and ordered whiskey. The barman, who was unusually noncommittal for one of his calling, served him at once, and hooking an elbow on the edge of the bar the lawman came about and faced the room.

At that moment two men sitting at a nearby table rose and hastily left the saloon. Rye frowned, the remembrance of Deputy Hoskins' words concerning the Dixon family and their desire for vengeance on Asa Metzgar rising in his mind.

He shrugged off the thought. Neither of the two fit the descriptions the deputy had given him. Likely their sudden departure at his arrival was mere coincidence. Too, Hoskins had said there'd been no signs of the Dixons in Prescott for some time. In all probability when Metzgar had disappeared they had given up.

Treating himself to another drink of the liquor, Rye paid off, left the place, and headed for the hotel. He wanted to reread the letter he had received from the Chief Marshal once more, get everything straight in his mind. Then he'd turn in, get a few hours' sleep and be ready to quietly leave town shortly after midnight, when the likelihood of being noticed would be very small.

The pair he'd seen in Kelly's might not have been the Dixons but there could be others who had a grudge against Metzgar, the Hanging Judge, and, recognizing Rye as a lawman, suspected his presence in Prescott had something to do with the jurist.

That was only a possibility, but John Rye had learned from experience that possibilities all too often became actualities, and he was in a profession where it never paid to take anything for granted.

4

Rye downed another drink and then, lighting up one of his stogies, strolled casually to the doorway and stepped out onto the landing. Immediately he swept the street with a sharp, probing glance. A grim sort of satisfaction stirred him. The two men who had hastily departed the saloon when he entered were standing in the shade of a store building almost opposite.

Anger lifted within the lawman. If the pair had something on their minds, either relative to Judge Metzgar or to a personal matter concerning him, Rye wanted to know about it. He'd not have them skulking about furtively eyeing his every move from the shadows.

He took a step toward the street, intending to cross over and confront the two men, but at that moment Charley Hoskins suddenly appeared a short distance away on the sidewalk.

"You get all fixed up?" the deputy asked, halting before the marshal.

Rye made no reply but ducked his head at the pair on the opposite side of the street. At once they wheeled about and hurried along the side of the store building next to which they had been standing.

"You know them?"

Hoskins frowned, shook his head. "Sure don't, but I've seen them around town a couple of times. Never heard their names. They give you some trouble?"

"No, they just seem to be taking a mighty big interest in me. Set me to wondering if they'd got wind of what I'm here for. You talk to anybody about it?"

"Hell no, Marshal!" Hoskins replied in an injured tone. "I ain't said a word to nobody . . . Now, if you want I'll run them in and we can ask them what they're doing here."

"I'll appreciate it—"

"Could be just a couple of pilgrims just riding through—and they might know who you are and are just wanting to get a good look at the Doomsday Marshal. You're a mite famous, you know."

John Rye smiled faintly but the slight tightening of his jaw reflected a dislike of the term. He had never particularly liked the appellation that had been hung on him by outlaws as well as ordinary citizens. And while he did nothing to discourage its use, as he felt it did aid him to some degree in his pursuing outlaws, he would have been just as happy if everyone forgot it.

Standing quietly on the sidewalk which fronted the saloon, Rye continued to stare off into the direction the two men had taken. He had removed his fringed jacket, and was dressed now in flat-crowned brown hat, blue shirt and bandanna, brown cord pants and dusty black stovepipe boots. Despite the late-afternoon heat he looked cool, utterly calm and controlled, and the lethal look of him was almost threatening.

Hoskins' features sobered. "I didn't mean no harm, Marshal, calling you that. Figured everybody did."

"Everybody does—except my friends," Rye said. "Like to count you among the few I have."

Hoskins bobbed happily. "Sure pleasure me to be one! I know how it is with a man wearing a star. Folks just sort of hold back, like they were afraid to get friendly. They make a lawman feel about as welcome as a coyote in a hen house."

"For sure," Rye agreed, "but I reckon that's part of what we're getting paid for. If you come up with anything special on those two men I'll be at the hotel."

"Aim to see what I can find out about them. Meant to ask you earlier: how about taking supper with me and the missus this evening? We'd be mighty pleased to have you."

Rye removed the stogie from his mouth, smiled and shook his head. "Pleasure would be all mine, Charley, but I just had a big meal—and I'm needing sleep. Figure to turn in early. Obliged to you, however."

Hoskins, visibly disappointed, shrugged. "I see, but if you change your mind come on over. We live in the house right behind the jail."

"Thanks, I'll remember the invitation . . . Say howdy to the sheriff for me," Rye said and, turning, headed for the hotel.

An hour or so past midnight John Rye gathered up his few belongings and quickly left the hostelry. The clerk was nowhere to be seen and insofar as the lawman knew his departure went unnoticed.

Except for the saloons—Kelly's and several smaller establishments—the business houses along the street were dark and quiet as Rye made his way to the livery stable. Reaching there he found the door closed with the hasp in place but there was no padlock, only a carriage bolt serving as a pin, and removing it, he opened the door and entered the odorous, pitch dark structure.

In the dim light from the outside he saw a lantern hanging on the wall, and striking a match he closed the door, lit the lantern and looked around for his horses. They were in the two front stalls just as the hostler had promised, and hanging the light on a convenient peg he saddled and bridled the chestnut, then strapped his pack back on the bay.

When they were ready he extinguished the lantern and opened the door, and with the troublesome thought of the two men who had showed so much interest in him still weighing on his mind, had a long, careful look up and down the street. He had heard nothing from Charley Hoskins but he took no real assurance from that.

The town looked deserted just as it had appeared earlier, and the only sounds—the tinkling of a piano and an occasional burst of laughter—were coming from Kelly's. Leading the horses into the open, he shut the door, replaced the pin in the hasp, leaving all just as he'd found it. Then, swinging up into the saddle, with the pack horse trailing the chestnut closely, he struck a course due west out of the settlement.

Rye was certain he had not been seen leaving Prescott, but, thorough as always, he continued on that route for an hour or so and then cut off the trail into a dense stand of scrub oak. Leaving the saddle, he made his way forward through the growth to where he had a good view of the Clear Springs road.

Almost immediately he caught the sound of horses coming toward him—two, he thought judging by the dust-muted hoof beats. That guess proved to be correct for shortly the animals, riders hunched forward on the saddle, came into view. An oath slipped from the lawman's lips. It was the pair who had been watching him in town. Waiting until they were abreast the patch of scrub oak, he stepped out into the center of the road. His abrupt appearance brought the horses up short, almost throwing one of the riders, who had evidently been dozing, from the saddle.

Hand resting on the butt of his gun, Rye considered the two men coldly. After a moment he drew his weapon and motioned with it.

"Climb down," he directed in a flat tone.

The pair complied slowly. One of the two, a young man in ordinary range clothing, features indeterminate in the pale starlight, raised his hands overhead quickly. The other, somewhat older, tall, lean, wearing a dirt-streaked gray shirt, black leather vest, scarred boots and faded denim pants, reacted more sullenly.

"What's on your minds?" Rye demanded as the pair faced him. "You been eyeballing me ever since I walked into Kelly's Saloon, now you're dogging my tracks. Want to know why."

"We ain't dogging you, Marshal," the shorter of the two said. "Just happens we're heading east looking for jobs. Ain't no law against that, is there?"

They knew he was a lawman. Rye's suspicion grew.

"That right? You looking for a job, too?"

"Reckon I am—"

Rye continued to consider the pair coldly. Then, "You got names?"

"I'm Shorty Pedgett," the younger man said. "My partner there's called—"

"John Smith," the tall man cut in.

Pedgett glanced frowningly at Smith and shrugged. "We only met a couple of days ago. Happened to be heading in the same direction and looking for the same thing so we just naturally throwed in together."

"Why were you keeping an eye on me back in town?"

Pedgett hesitated for a few moments and then shrugged. "My partner here said you was that big lawman they call the Doomsday Marshal. I was wanting to get a good look at you."

Rye's attention shifted to the older man. "How'd you know who I was?"

Smith turned his head, spat into the flinty gravel alongside the trail. "Seen you down Nogales way. Recollected you from there. You were handing over some Mexican outlaw to the *federales.*"

Rye recalled the incident. It had taken place a little more than a year ago. He stirred impatiently. Maybe the two men were just pilgrims, one of whom was curious. That damned Doomsday Marshal thing could be a nuisance at times.

"If you're heading east why don't we just all ride along together?" Shorty Pedgett said cheerfully. He had lowered his arms, was now standing straddle-legged with thumbs hooked in his gun belt.

Rye shook his head. He wanted no trail partners and wasn't interested in making friends. Pedgett and Smith, if that was their real names, might be who and what they claimed to be—and maybe they weren't. Considering what Deputy Hoskins back in Prescott had told him about the enemies Asa Metzgar had accumulated in the area, they very well could be among those, like the Dixons, who were out seeking vengeance, and either suspecting or learning somehow that he was there to meet the judge and escort him out of the country, figured to follow along in the belief that he would lead them to Metzgar.

"No, you best ride on," he said, not holstering his

gun but letting it hang at his side. "Aim to make camp and get myself a few minutes' shut-eye." He paused, watched Smith and Pedgett climb back onto their horses. "Hope you find yourselves jobs. Little scarce, I hear tell."

"It's the truth," Shorty said, "but we're hoping it'll change. I'm about busted flat . . . *Adios.*"

"So long," Rye answered as the pair rode off into the star-bright night.

The lawman waited until the men were no longer in sight and then returned to his horses. Mounting up, Rye cut back to the trail and then veered south. If Shorty Pedgett and the sour-faced man who called himself John Smith intended to double back expecting to find him rolled up tight in his blanket, they had another guess coming.

5

Rye reached Clear Springs, pocketed in a grassy swale surrounded by tall pines, around the middle of the afternoon. Approaching from the southeast, he drew rein at the edge of the settlement and had his look at the thin scatter of store buildings and houses. The town existed no doubt for the sole purpose of supplying the ranchers and homesteaders in the immediate area, since there were no crisscrossing main roads that would enable it to survive.

Studying the settlement's one dusty main street, the lawman watched as a stout, sunbonneted woman made an appearance about midway along, crossed over and entered one of the two general stores. Then, seeing no other activity of interest or signs of Shorty Pedgett and John Smith, he rode on.

The livery barn stood at the opposite end of the street. It bore no name on its false front other than "Stable," and leading the chestnut with the little bay trailing along behind, Rye pointed for it. Along the short distance he took note of the business concerns. A saloon bearing the somewhat grandiose name the Golden Slipper stood next to the stable while directly opposite was Cable's Hotel. Strung out in irregular sequence elsewhere along the dusty, deserted street were various other establishments: a feed store, harness shop, men's and ladies' clothing, and in a somewhat lengthy, slant-roofed structure were a doctor, a

lawyer and the town marshal. Set back somewhat
from it was a church alongside which was a parsonage,
and beyond that a fenced-in cemetery.

It was a small, cozy-looking little village with a backdrop of tall pine and fir trees, much shrubbery, color-
ful flowers and lush green grass. The spring that gave
the town its name sent a quiet silver ribbon of water
winding its way along the fringe of the settlement.

It would be pleasant to someday retire in a small,
out-of-the-way town such as Clear Springs, Rye
thought as he rode slowly down the street. It was a
place where he could feel free of tension, be shut of
riding endless trails, one where he could go quietly
about living the rest of his life. But the coming of that
day was a long time off, assuming he lived to see it.
Too, he was not yet thirty years of age, and if all went
according to plan, he was only halfway to the day
when he'd feel he should hang up his gun.

And by then Clear Springs would have changed,
would have become larger and less appealing—or
could have disappeared altogether. He'd have to find
a settlement that appealed to him, and chances were
it would be in another territory or state. He liked to
think it would be Arizona, however; he was partial to
that part of the country.

Rye grinned and shrugged away his thoughts. Being
a lawman he was a fool to be laying plans for thirty
years or so in the future. He'd be smart to concentrate
on staying alive during the intervening time and make
his choice of a final homeland when—and if—that
time ever came.

Veering the chestnut wide of the livery barn, he
casually circled the squat structure and, entering the
trees and brushy growth beyond it, angled toward the

church. The chief marshal's letter had said Metzgar was hiding out in the home of a preacher named Mathews, and since there appeared to be but one church in Clear Springs, Mathews no doubt was its minister.

Swinging wide around the house, nestled against the steepled church, the lawman came into it from the rear and halted behind a hedge of lilacs. He doubted anyone had paid him any mind when he entered the settlement but there was always the chance someone did, and if so, he was making certain not to reveal his ultimate destination.

Securely tying the chestnut to one of the bushes in the hedge, Rye moved past the lilacs and, crossing a small yard in which various vegetables were growing, made his way to the back of the house. There were no other structures nearby and he felt certain his presence was not being noted. He raised his hand and rapped sharply on the screen door.

Somewhere inside a chair scraped across the floor. A few moments later a tall, red-faced man with thick overhanging brows stood framed in the doorway. He was dressed in dark pants and coat and the collarless shirt he wore was snowy white.

"Yes?" he said in a deep voice.

"You Silas Mathews?" the lawman asked.

The minister nodded. "I am. What can I do for you?"

"I'm here to get Judge Metzgar. I'm United States Marshal John Rye," the lawman said and exhibited his star.

Mathews relaxed visibly. "Come in, come in," he said, unhooking the door and holding it open. "To say I'm glad to see you would be putting it mildly."

Rye stepped inside, drew up short as he caught a glimpse of a man, rifle in his hands, standing in the far side of the room.

"Sort of gathered that from your welcome," the marshal said, and nodded to the slight, tense figure with the rifle. "Howdy, Judge. You can put that gun down. I'm here as a friend."

Metzgar, in his mid-sixties, was a thin, wizened man with a heavily lined face. His hair was white, as were his mustache, goatee and thick brows, from beneath which he studied the marshal with small dark eyes. He had a quick, nervous way to him and he seemed angered rather than relieved at John Rye's arrival.

"Took you long enough to get here," he said irritably. "Expected you a week ago."

"Had other things to do," Rye said coolly. "No chance to get here any sooner."

"Well, I'm mighty glad you've arrived," Mathews said as if endeavoring to ease the bristling anger that had sprung up between the two men. "I was afraid some of the judge's enemies were going to spot him."

"How long's he been hiding out here?"

"Couple of weeks, more or less."

"There been anybody around looking for him?"

"Not exactly by here," Metzgar said, coming into the conversation, "but the Dixons are in town. Don't know how, but somehow they learned I was in town. Been skulking about trying to find out where I'm staying for the last three days."

"The Dixons," Rye repeated thoughtfully. "Heard about them from the deputy in Prescott. Have you seen them or do you only think they're here?"

"Oh, they're around, all right!" Metzgar said, laying the rifle across a close-by table. "I saw Gar Dixon and that boy of his, Devon, coming out of the saloon only yesterday. I expect Hillman was somewhere close."

Rye rubbed at the stubble on his chin. "Sure like to know how they found out you were here in Clear Springs."

"We tried to keep it quiet but word could've leaked out somehow—or maybe I was seen traveling in this direction. Point is they know I'm here and that poses the question of how you're going to get me out without them knowing."

"Something I'll need to do some figuring on, but don't fret about it, I'll manage."

Metzgar swore softly and, taking a pint bottle of whiskey from his coat pocket, helped himself to a swallow.

"Was expecting the governor to send at least a squad of soldiers to get me out of this town," he said wearily. "Hardly see how one man, even you, Rye, can get the job done."

The marshal smiled dryly. "Wasn't sure you remembered me, Judge," he said, and then added: "But like I said, don't worry about it. I'll get you through."

Metzgar shook his head doubtfully. "Seems I have no choice but depend on you."

"That's right . . . Coming here from Prescott I ran into a couple of riders headed this way. Had a hunch they were headed for Clear Springs."

"You think they were looking for me?" Metzgar asked.

"Hard to answer that. Could be they were out to get me."

"What did they look like?" the judge pressed, a deep frown on his narrow face as he settled onto one of the chairs. Dressed in a worn brown suit, black sateen shirt, limp white string tie, flat-heeled boots, he looked rumpled and near exhaustion from worry.

"One was young—called himself Shorty Pedgett. Other'n was older, probably in his mid-forties. Hard-looking, quiet man. Didn't talk much. Was riding a sorrel horse and called himself John Smith, which I figure was a lie."

Metzgar was silent as he considered the information. Somewhere in the settlement a jackass brayed and outside in the garden a dozen or so sparrows chattered busily as they foraged about.

"Neither one sounds familiar to me," the jurist said finally, "but I can't say for certain. Been so many men come up before me in my time as a judge that I can't expect to remember them all."

"Seems you ought to recollect the names of the ones out to kill you," Rye commented dryly.

Metzgar sighed deeply. "Maybe that sounds easy to you, but I can't, mainly because I don't actually know who-all's got it in their minds to square up what they consider a wrong that I've done them. There are a few, yes—like the Dixons. There are others, I'm sure, but just who they are I can't even guess . . . What are your plans for getting me out of here?"

"Think I've already said I'll have to look around, size up the situation, then make plans," Rye replied and turned to Mathews. "There anybody else at all knows the judge has been living here with you? Your wife's bound to be one."

"I'm a widower," Mathews said. "There's a woman who comes by once a week, housekeeper, and she does a bit of cooking. Expect she's noticed there's somebody else around although she's never seen the judge. He hides out in the yard when she's here. Other than her I can't think of anybody that would know."

"Best we figure there is," the marshal said, walking to the door and glancing out. "I believe in playing it safe at a time like this."

Metzgar got to his feet. Nervous and filled with misgivings he stroked his goatee agitatedly. "I think I'd best stay right here, wait for the governor to send those soldiers—"

"They won't be coming," Rye cut in. "I'll be all you need: two riders will attract a lot less attention than a squad of soldiers. Long as you do as you're told I'll get you to Nebraska alive."

Metzgar was still unconvinced. "Just don't see how one man, even you, can do it," he said, voicing an earlier complaint.

"Just you be ready to leave after dark," the lawman said, his tone impatient. He turned to Mathews. "I'm a bit low on grub. You mind picking up a few things at the store for me? Don't think anybody saw me ride in, and I'd like to keep it that way."

"Just give me a list," the minister said as Rye handed him a gold eagle.

"What'll you be doing?" Metzgar asked.

"Getting the horses ready," the marshal said after naming off the items Mathews was to purchase. "Where's yours?"

"In the shed out back—"

"I'll saddle and bridle him. You get your gear together. We'll be leaving on short notice."

John Rye was not sure just how simple their departure would be, considering the fact that the Dixons were in town. And he had to consider the two men he'd met on the trail, Pedgett and Smith. They could

be as determined to find Asa Metzgar as were the
Dixons—or they could have no interest in him at all.
That was what made the job more difficult—the not
knowing for sure.

6

Gar Dixon lifted the battered old tin pot with its load of boiling chicory off the fire and set it on the ground nearby. The combination of salt pork, beans, potatoes and onions in the skillet had finished cooking also, and the chunks of bread he'd placed on the rocks containing the fire were now toasted to a warm brown.

"Come on and eat," he called to the two men squatting on their heels in the doorway of the abandoned shack where they had quartered for the past week.

The pair got indifferently to their feet and crossed to the fire where Gar was spooning out a measure of the mixture into tin plates.

"What's in it this time, Pa—salt pork and spuds again?" the younger man asked.

"It's fitten to eat," Gar snapped. "Just you keep remembering your brothers are where they can't eat nothing."

"I reckon they're where they plain don't need nothing," the boy said, taking up one of the plates. Selecting a spoon and a piece of bread, he drew off to one side and sat down on an empty nail keg.

Gar studied him briefly and shrugged. "Devon, I sure can't figure you sometimes. Here we are getting powerful close to finding that goddamn murdering judge that strung up your brothers, and all you can do is bellyache. Seems to me you ought to be thinking about your bounden duty to even the score for them. Ain't that right, Saul?"

Saul Hillman, a slim, sharp-featured man with dark eyes, nodded woodenly as he found himself a seat near Devon.

"Yeh, reckon so, Gar, but I sure would like to taste something besides salt pork and beans."

"Why can't I sort of slip into town and buy us something else to eat, Pa? Some red meat, like beef or ham. And maybe some corn. Ain't nobody around here knows me."

"Can't be for sure of that," the elder Dixon said, filling his own plate and then pouring himself a cup of the chicory coffee. "And we'd sure be fools to take the chance of somebody spotting us now that we're this close."

"If we are," Hillman said, "we ain't seen hide nor hair of him."

"He's bound to be around here. That hostler in Prescott said Metzgar headed this way when he left, and he was running like a scared rabbit—and this here's the only town he could have gone to, there ain't being no other'n anywhere in this part of the country."

"Could've just kept on riding," Devon said between mouthfuls of the greasy fare. "You ever think of that, Pa? He just maybe rode right on through here, not stopping atall."

"Ain't likely," Gar replied with a shake of his head. "That jasper I talked to in the saloon said he'd seen a fellow fitting Metzgar's description headed this way about two weeks ago—and he never seen him leave."

"But he ain't seen nothing of him since, neither," Devon Dixon pointed out, reaching for a cup to fill with the chicory, "so that don't mean nothing. Metzgar could've rode out and that fellow never seen him 'cause he couldn't've been watching all the time."

Gar chewed thoughtfully on a piece of pork for a time. He shrugged. "Maybe so, but I've got a hunch he's still around here hiding out somewhere."

"Kind of hard to believe that," Hillman said. "I'd figure a man would keep right on going if he was scared."

Gar, cup halfway to his mouth, paused, listened as the beat of a running horse along the street drew his attention. Half rising, he watched the rider pass by and then, satisfied that it was no one of interest to him, settled back down.

"I expect that's the reason he wouldn't keep on going," Gar said, taking a swallow of the strong, bitter liquid. "He's plenty scared. Now, we ain't the only folks looking to revenge our kin. I'll bet there's a dozen or more hunting him, which is why we got to stay right on his trail and get to him first."

"Well, I'm hoping that'll be pretty soon," Saul Hillman said wearily. "I got to—"

"You're welcome to pull out anytime," Gar said angrily. "Them two boys wasn't nothing but nephews of your'n, the sons of your poor dead sister and me, so you ain't got such a big stake in finding that murdering bastard and killing him like me and Devon have. Now you feel free to pack up and leave anytime you get the notion."

Hillman made no reply, simply chewed slowly on the chunk of salt pork and other bits of the stew. Nearby Devon finished his plate and, taking no more from the spider, contented himself with dunking his piece of bread in his cup of chicory.

"We've been watching for several days, Pa, and

there ain't been no sign of him," the boy said. "I can't figure how you can be so sure he's here."

"Got a feeling, that's how—a real deep feeling."

"What about them two that come in yesterday? They kept on riding. Anybody tell you about them?"

"That short-legged kid and the jasper in the counterjumper hat riding the sorrel? Seen them myself. Watched them from the back of the livery stable. Hell, seeing a body come and go in this burg ain't no chore. Only one road in and one road out."

"But there's a God's plenty of cover all around the place," Devon said. "Seems to me it'd be easy to sneak in and out without being spotted."

"Unless he had to stop for grub or a drink, or maybe something else. Anyway, we're chewing the cud for nothing. We're staying right here till we either root old Metzgar out or find out for goddamn sure he ain't around."

A woman in a red-wheeled buggy drawn by a small white mare passed by, heading, no doubt, for one of the town's stores. A ragged-looking dog trotted contentedly along under the vehicle, ignoring the dust stirred up by the horse's hooves, but enjoying the shade cast by the light rig.

"Hell, why don't we just start going from house to house knocking on the door and seeing if Metzgar's inside. Bound to turn him up that way," Devon suggested. "It'd sure beat this setting around waiting."

Gar swore, tossed the last of his coffee substitute aside. "Now that's a real smart idea, ain't it? You think he'd come to the door asking to know what we want? Or maybe you think the friend he's hiding with would just admit the bastard's there and invite us in? Use your head, son!"

The elder Dixon, finished with the meal, drew a plug of tobacco from his pocket and, opening the jackknife he carried, carved a bit off one corner. He hadn't shaved in over a week, and the beard covering the lower part of his face was jet-black and glistened in the strong sunlight.

Gar had dropped everything after Asa Metzgar had found his two young sons guilty and hanged them. From the moment the trap of the scaffold had opened and they had dropped to their deaths, one thing only had become uppermost in his mind: avenge the boys, kill Asa Metzgar. What matter if the evidence proved Price and Cord had killed the two Caffrey girls and their mother? Metzgar had no call to murder his boys —and he had to pay for it.

Gar had gone straight to the hotel in Chino Valley, where the executions had taken place, with the sole purpose in mind of killing the judge. But Metzgar had gone through similar situations before and had departed hours earlier, with no clue as to where he was going.

Gar Dixon didn't give it up there. Leaving the farm in the care of a hired hand, and with Devon and Saul Hillman siding him, he set out to run down the Hanging Judge, as he'd later discovered Metzgar was called. He got close twice but never quite caught up with the man, who took great pains to keep his itinerary secret. But finally, again in Prescott, Gar got a lead. Metzgar had been there, stayed briefly and ridden on, taking the road east. He'd been in a hell of a hurry, the hostler who'd noted his passage had said.

That was almost two weeks ago, and Dixon, getting the tip only two days after the judge had ridden out of the capital city, had followed immediately. But so far it had proved to be a dead end. Neither he nor Devon nor Hillman had been able to turn up any solid proof that Metzgar was in the settlement.

Maybe Saul and Devon were right. Maybe they were wasting time hanging around Clear Springs. Metzgar could have ridden on unnoticed by the people he'd talked to and at that hour was getting farther and farther away. Still Gar had that gut feeling that he wasn't wrong, that the hated Hanging Judge who had snapped the necks and taken the lives of his two young sons was there.

"Reckon we best get working, see if we can turn up something," he said, getting to his feet. In the shadowy area fronting the shack he looked heavier, broader, than he actually was, while the hard-set lines of his unforgiving features were as if cut in stone.

"Devon, you keep hanging around that general store. Could be he'll show up there—but you keep out of sight. Saul, keep an eye on the livery stable and that saloon like you've been doing."

"Where'll you be?" Devon asked.

"Aim to sort of roam around, watching the homes. There ain't many. I'm going to spend some time looking at that preacher's house, too. Be just like Metzgar to hole up in his place—there or the town marshal's."

"What about that woman that we see coming and going from the preacher's? Maybe she could tell us something about anybody new coming to town," Hillman suggested.

"That's a right smart idea. Whichever one of us sees her, stop her and do some asking—but don't kick up no ruckus. Sure don't want the local lawdog horning in."

7

"Ready to travel?" Rye asked, glancing through the window of the parsonage to the yard outside. It was full dark, and lamps were showing in the houses and buildings along Clear Springs' lone street.

Metzgar, sitting at the kitchen table where he, Silas Mathews and John Rye were having a last cup of coffee, shook his head.

"No, can't say as I am. Still think it best I wait for the government to send soldiers to get me to Nebraska—not just one man," he said sullenly.

"Forget the soldiers. Told you once they won't be coming. I'm all you're going to get; make up your mind to that," the lawman snapped.

Mathews considered Rye thoughtfully. "I know your reputation—that is, I've heard about you and I believe you're an able man—but do you think you can get the judge home without trouble?"

"What I've been ordered to do—and I aim to do it . . . Let's go, Metzgar."

The jurist got slowly to his feet. "Seems I don't have a choice," he said and, going into a room off the kitchen, returned shortly wearing a coat and hat and carrying his blanket roll.

"Out the back," Rye said. "Dark enough now. Nobody'll see us . . . Obliged to you, Reverend, for doing my buying for me; just didn't figure it'd be smart to let myself be seen."

"The Dixons know you?" Metzgar asked, halting.

"Don't think so, but I can't take any chances on it. So long; obliged to you for the favors," the marshal added, turning to Mathews.

"Glad to help," the minister answered. "Good luck, Asa," he said, nodding to Metzgar.

The judge shrugged. "Expect I'll be needing it," he said and, with no further word to the man who had given him shelter and concealment, moved off toward the shed where the horses waited.

Rye considered the shadowy figure of the man for a few moments and glanced at Mathews. "Don't know if he remembered to thank you for taking him on or not. If he didn't, I'm doing it now. Want to thank you for the government, too."

Mathews' thin shoulders stirred. "Was nothing. I felt sorry for the man. He has no friends—not a single one in this whole world—and he's worried and has a lot on his conscience . . . Good luck to you—and God be with you both."

"We're going to need somebody's help, that's for damn sure!" Metzgar's voice, deep and filled with bitterness, came unexpectedly from the darkness. Rye had thought the judge was beyond earshot but apparently he was not.

The lawman smiled at Mathews. "Obliged to you," he said and crossed to his horse. Climbing up into the saddle he cast a critical glance at Metzgar, then cut the chestnut around and headed out of the yard, followed immediately by the bay packhorse with Metzgar bringing up the rear.

"I'm not riding back here eating those animals' dust," he declared peevishly.

"You're welcome to come up here beside me," the marshal said patiently.

The long, thirty-day journey with Metzgar that lay ahead was going to be one he'd not soon forget, Rye realized as they moved on into the night. He swore softly again at the ill luck causing him to be assigned the chore of conducting the hated Hanging Judge to his home safely. He would gladly swap jobs with any lawman in the land regardless of what it might entail.

Reaching the trees beyond the end of Silas Mathews' yard, Rye veered west, picking up a fairly well used trail that bore directly into that direction. At once Asa Metzgar protested.

"What the hell are you going this way for? We ought to be riding east—for New Mexico."

Rye pulled to a halt and faced the judge. In the pale light his features were taut, angry. "Best we get this straight right now. I'm the one heading up this party. I pick the trails we'll follow, and you'll keep your mouth shut and do what I tell you!"

"But this is the wrong way to Nebr—"

"Nebraska's east and north of us—I know that—but if your friends the Dixons are onto us, or maybe Pedgett and Smith are hanging around trying to get a bead on you, I aim to shed them fast as possible. We'll go west for a spell, then swing north, and after a time turn east. That satisfy you?"

Metzgar pulled his round, black hat farther down on his head and bobbed. "All right with me. Just wanted to know what we were doing," he said and, as they moved on, took a pint bottle of whiskey from the inside pocket of his coat and had a quick drink. "You aim to ride all night?"

"Likely," the lawman replied. The farther they got

from Clear Springs before daylight, the better he'd feel.

They rode steadily on the bright moon and starlit night, wending their way through the tall pines and other mountain growth. Coyotes barked from the distance, and once their passage frightened a horned owl that glided off into the night, its broad wings making a quiet swishing sound. Occasionally through the growth they could see the yellow glow of lamps in the windows of some homesteader's or miner's cabin, and twice they heard riders passing directly across in front of them.

Rye kept a close watch on Metzgar, who appeared to doze most of the time, as he didn't want the elderly man to fall from the saddle, injure himself and cause them trouble and delay.

As they pressed on he wondered about the Dixons, if they had actually been in Clear Springs, or whether Metzgar, gripped by fear, had just imagined it. It wasn't the Dixons that disturbed the lawman, however, but the pair he had encountered on the road from Prescott—John Smith and Shorty Pedgett. They were in the area, that was certain, for he had seen them, and that fact bothered him more than the possibility of the Dixons being on their trail.

But neither the pair he'd met that had aroused his suspicions nor the Dixons should be of any concern now. By taking the route he had, he would have put them well off in the wrong direction, assuming they had some idea of where he and Metzgar were going— a town called Plattesville in Nebraska. It occurred to Rye then that if they did know, all the careful maneuvering he employed could be for nothing, as they could simply ride on ahead and be waiting for the judge at his home settlement, or perhaps someplace nearby. He'd have to bear that in mind, Rye thought, and not take Asa Metzgar into an ambush.

A short time later he decided they had ridden west far enough, and with Metzgar asleep in his saddle and accordingly unaware of any change, Rye swung due north. They'd continue on that course for a time, at least until they were a good distance from the trail that led east out of Clear Springs, and then change again, turning into that direction. If the Dixons or John Smith and Pedgett were on the east road, they would then be miles to the south.

First light found Rye and Metzgar moving through a narrow canyon. A small creek flowed along its gravelly floor and, coming to a place where some preceding pilgrim had made camp, the marshal halted. At once Metzgar roused.

"What's the matter?" he asked hurriedly. "What are you stopping for?"

"Breakfast, and give the horses a bit of rest," Rye replied. As Mathews had said, the judge was nervous but the lawman hadn't realized just how bad off he really was.

"You think we're far enough from Clear Springs to pull up?"

"I reckon so," Rye said. "Whether we are or not we have to. Have to spell the horses—and I'm hungry."

Metzgar muttered something under his breath and climbed down from his saddle. He was riding a well-built bay gelding that had weathered the long miles from the town only fairly well. Crossing to the packhorse, Rye removed the grub sack along with the one in which he carried cooking equipment. Rye dropped back to the blackened circle of rocks that had served as a firebox for the previous pilgrim.

"You can either see to watering and feeding the horses," he said, laying down the sack, "or you can do the cooking."

Metzgar stared at him for a long breath and then wordlessly took up the reins of the horses and led them grudgingly to a place along the stream below the camp. Rye smiled wryly. He'd get damn little help from the man called the Hanging Judge, that was sure.

A tall pine, a victim of lightning at some time in the past, lay nearby, affording an ample and convenient supply of dry wood. Filling the coffeepot with water from the creek, Rye built a fire and set the blackened container over the flames to heat, after which he prepared a meal of thick-sliced bacon, chunks of potatoes, warmed bread and honey, all to be topped off with preserved peaches.

When it was ready he called to Metzgar, sitting on a large rock a dozen yards upstream. The jurist rose and indifferently made his way to where Rye had portioned out the meat and potatoes onto plates.

"Is this the kind of grub we'll be eating?" Metzgar grumbled, taking up his plate. "Looks like a greasy mess."

Rye shrugged. "It's what you'll get while we're on the trail. If you figure you can do a better job of cooking, the job's sure yours."

"Most anything'll beat this," Metzgar said.

The marshal smiled in a humorless way. "Like I said, the job's yours if you don't like my cooking," he drawled and, taking up a piece of the bread, placed it on his plate, filled his cup with steaming coffee and drew off to one side. Metzgar could eat or he could go hungry; the next meal that would be put together would be at dark—or later.

The sky was brightening in the east, and a low-lying bank of dark-bellied clouds was beginning to collect along the southern horizon. They could expect rain before the day was over, Rye guessed; he'd best remember to get his slicker out and have it handy—something he'd also remind the judge to do. Or maybe he'd just let Metzgar, who seemed unwilling to take advice of any kind, find out the hard way that clouds to the south almost invariably meant wet weather.

In the trees behind them camp robber jays were quarreling noisily, and well off to the north a dog was barking. There'd be a miner's cabin somewhere up there, or perhaps it was a homesteader toughing out the cold winters and not-too-kind summers, he supposed.

Rye shifted his attention to Metzgar. The judge was picking at his plate of food, selecting small pieces of the potatoes and bacon. He had not helped himself yet to either the bread or the coffee.

"Going to be a long day," the lawman said, rising and crossing to the grub sacks and picking up the Mason jar of peaches. Dumping about half of the fruit onto his plate, he offered the remainder to the jurist. "Eat some of these pickled peaches. They'll help cut the grease."

Metzgar set his plate down and shook his head. "No, thanks. I'd as soon do without," he said and, drawing a pipe and tobacco from his coat pocket, began to fill the charred bowl with shreds of the weed. Nudging his almost-full plate with the toe of his boot, he added: "This is another reason I had hoped the government would send the Army after me. A man can eat decent food when he's with them."

"Well, I'm not the Army," Rye said disgustedly and got to his feet. Tossing the leavings on his plate off into the brush where the jays and small varmints could feed on them, he turned about and faced Metzgar.

"If you're going to be harping and bellyaching like this for the next month, I'd as soon we'd head back to Clear Springs and let you hole up with that preacher while you talk the government into sending some soldiers for you. I didn't want this job in the first place, so—"

Metzgar, his pipe filled and a match posed ready to be struck, cut in hurriedly. "No, never said I wanted to do that—only that I was hoping it would be that way—that the Army would come, I mean."

The marshal watched Metzgar strike the match, hold it to the bowl of his pipe and puff the tobacco into life. He supposed he should be a little more patient with the judge, but he was finding it hard to do.

"They didn't, and they won't—so the smart thing you can do is forget about it. And I don't want to hear any more beefing about the grub, or the trail we take, or anything else. That clear?"

Metzgar's face darkened. He removed the pipe from between his teeth and fixed his sharp black eyes on Rye. "I won't stand to be talked to in that tone of voice, mister! If you think—"

"You'll listen to me and you'll do what I tell you—and you'll keep your mouth shut; else we head back to Clear Springs!" Rye snapped. "Hear?"

Metzgar stared at the lawman for a full minute and then, making no reply, turned away. Rye stepped forward quickly, caught the man by the shoulder and brought him back around. There had to be an under-standing between them, especially as to who was in charge, otherwise they could both get killed. Whether Metzgar ate or not was of no concern to the lawman.

Metzgar, startled, accustomed to having his own way and never being challenged, lost his grip on the pipe. It fell to the ground at his feet.

"Goddammit," he muttered and tried to pull away but Rye's grip was like a vise on his shoulder.

"I want an answer. Either we do it my way or not at all. I'm giving you a choice here and now."

Metzgar, face red, jaw set, swore again. "All right, it's your way."

"Means clear to Nebraska—till the minute I turn you over to the law there."

"Whatever you want," Metzgar said sullenly and, when the lawman released his hold, bent down and retrieved his pipe. Brushing dirt off the stem, he added: "I don't aim to give you any trouble."

But John Rye was paying no attention to the judge's words at that point. His eyes were reaching beyond him to a ridge a half mile distant where three riders were silhouetted against the hazy sky. Wheeling at once, the lawman ran to his horse and, obtaining the brass telescope he carried in his saddlebags, returned hurriedly to Metzgar. The judge had followed the line of his attention and was watching the riders, a frown tightening his features.

"Here," the marshal said, thrusting the glass into his hands. "Do you know who those men are?"

Metzgar studied the riders for only three or four moments and then nodded to Rye. "Yeh—they're the Dixons."

8

Taut, Rye took the telescope from Metzgar. He had hoped to get away from Clear Springs and head for Nebraska with no problems, but already something had gone wrong. Training the glass on the riders, he studied them carefully.

"How'd they know I'd be heading this direction?" Metzgar wondered. His voice was ragged and heavy with worry. "That preacher must've talked, damn him to h—"

"Doubt if it was him," Rye cut in, lowering the glass. "Maybe you mentioned it sometime when you were talking, or it could be that housekeeper of Mathews' did know you were there and let something slip that got to the Dixons. You said they were in Clear Springs."

"Could be but I didn't think she ever knew about me. But the hell with her; big thing now is, what do we do? They're going in the same direction, damn near on the same trail."

"We stay clear of them, that's all we'll have to do."

Metzgar shook his head impatiently at the simple answer. "I think the best thing we can do is to move on and circle in ahead of them; they're not traveling fast. Can pick us a good spot and when they show up, shoot them down."

Rye turned to the judge. "You talking about an ambush?"

"Exactly. We're both carrying revolvers, and you've got a shotgun. We can take care of the three of them with no trouble."

"You're talking cold-blooded murder," the marshal said in a tight voice. He was finding it hard to believe what he had heard. "You're a judge, the head of a court who is supposed to uphold the law, not break it."

"Be smart to get rid of them and—"

"I know you're a hard man," Rye continued, "but to come right out with a scheme to murder three men—"

"Why not? They're out to murder me. Let's get mounted and do what I said."

Rye shook his head. "We're not about to, Judge. The Dixons haven't done anything wrong, far as I can see. Talk is not something you kill a man for."

"They'll sure kill me if they get a chance—"

"It's my job to see they don't get that chance," the lawman said. "Load up, we're moving on."

At once he came about, crossed to the horses and led them into camp. Returning the unused food to the grub sack, rinsing the plates and pans in the stream and putting them back in their burlap container, he made ready to travel. Metzgar stood idly to one side, holding the bridle of his bay and watching Rye make preparations to leave.

The lawman suppressed the anger that stirred through him at the jurist's indifference, stepped up into the saddle, and, with no word to Metzgar, rode off. At once the judge mounted. Hurriedly catching up, he pressed in beside the lawman.

"Which way we going? You're not taking the same trail they are, are you? I've got a right to know!"

"North," Rye said, wasting no words.

"North? We've got to go east!"

"We will," the lawman said impatiently. "The Dixons are aiming to follow the Mogollon Rim Trail, hoping to find us in one of the towns along the way, I figure. We'll keep going north till we find a cross trail that'll take us to where we want to go."

"Sounds like we're doing a lot of unnecessary riding," Metzgar grumbled.

"Long way to Nebraska, Judge. We have to make the trip a jump at a time. Next stop we'll make for supplies will be Socorro, on the Rio Grande, in New Mexico territory."

"I know where it is," Metzgar said. "Won't that be where the Dixons will head for?"

"Could be, and again maybe they'll hit the river farther down. No way of knowing exactly; just have to guess and take our chances on me being right."

Metzgar swore, shifted on his saddle. "Not used to traveling this way. Used the stagecoach, or the train . . . How long will it take us to get to Socorro?"

"Having to swing north like we're doing, it'll mean ten, maybe twelve, days. Only been across this way once before and I don't remember exactly just what the country's like."

Rye had taken a stogie from his pocket case and was lighting up. Metzgar, following suit, drew out his pipe and tobacco and prepared a smoke. The sun was well on its way by that hour and the night's coolness had faded. Far to the south the dark clouds had thickened and were now higher in the sky, strengthening the promise of rain.

"Is it going to be mountains all the way?" Metzgar wondered.

"Just about—at least till we get to the St. Augustine

Flats, in New Mexico. About a two-day ride across them."

"We should've settled with the Dixons back there when we had a chance," Metzgar said; "saved us all this riding. Just how much are we losing coming into Socorro this way?"

"Day or so. We're circling around the north side of the mountains. The other trail—the one the Dixons are on—is to the south. It's shorter and easier traveling, I expect, but we won't lose much. Doubt if a day longer getting to Nebraska will make much difference."

"Suppose not, since it'll be safer."

Rye glanced at the jurist as the horses moved steadily on. He was somewhat surprised. For once Metzgar seemed to be in agreement with him. Up to that moment the judge had opposed just about everything he'd proposed to do.

"Our only choice, safer or not."

"Still think it would have been best to settle with the Dixons when we had the chance. I know the kind of a lawman you are, Rye. You never hold back on killing a man."

"Only if it becomes necessary," Rye said stiffly. "When I set out after an outlaw, I intend to bring him back alive to face whatever the court has against him. If he decides to put up a fight and use his gun, it's his choice, not mine."

"According to the record there seems to have been a plenty who chose to fight," Metzgar said dryly.

"They made the first move," the lawman said, his gaze reaching out over the grassy flats and low hills that lay ahead of them.

"Doesn't take much to kill a man," Metzgar said after a time.

Rye, not liking the conversation much, removed the stogie from his mouth, turned his head aside and spat.

"Not the way you do it—sentence a man to die and then have somebody else execute him. A bit different from facing a man with a gun in his hand who's bent on killing you."

"Not my place to execute, only judge whether the man deserves to live or not. That in itself is a heavy burden to bear. Having to always be right makes for a lot of loneliness."

The marshal shrugged in disgust. "You figure you're right every time?"

"Maybe not, but I think it's all for the good of the country, even if I happen to make a mistake and have the wrong man executed. The overall effect it has on outlaws and men who are considering taking up the trade is beneficial; makes them think twice about becoming a criminal. The end justifies the means, I say. Don't you agree?"

"No," Rye said flatly. "I hold no truck with outlaws and I figure they're due everything they've got coming; but hanging an innocent man goes against everything the law stands for. You can't call that justice!"

"The way I see it the law and justice are two different things. A man has to balance one against the other and do whatever is necessary, regardless."

Rye stirred in his saddle. They were crossing a broad meadow and the horses were slowing every few yards to snatch up a mouthful of the knee-high grass that covered the land.

"Can see how you earned your nickname," he said after a bit.

"A hanging judge? I'm not ashamed of it. Truth is just the opposite: I'm proud of it. Outlaws who come up before me know what they can expect, and I like to believe my reputation has caused a lot of men to think hard before they committed a crime."

John Rye had no reply to that. He reckoned what Metzgar said was true: a reputation for being a hard, no-nonsense lawman had often been of help to him, and he supposed it would work the same for a man who sat in court and handed down judgment on others. But to hang an innocent man and think little of it, soothing his conscience by telling himself that it was for the good of all—that was hard to swallow.

As the days passed they rode steadily on, making their way through narrow canyons and broad valleys, crossing stretches of flats on which the grass grew green and tall, and along slopes where late-summer flowers laid broad splashes of vivid color. The rains came and passed on, refreshing the land as well as them, but never with such fierceness as to be an inconvenience.

They talked but little after that first day, each man having listened to and made his assessment of his companion, and words passing between them during those subsequent days had to do mainly with the duties of making camp, eating, and caring for the horses.

They crossed the vast, seemingly endless expanse of forsaken land known as the St. Augustine Flats, sixty miles long and forty wide, Rye recalled someone had told him; spent one night at the small settlement at its eastern edge; and continued on through the broken country beyond it for Socorro. Rye had figured about right: they were down to the last of their supplies, and they would reach the town just in time to stock up.

"We about there?" Metzgar asked wearily. "I'm sure saddle-sore; worst I can ever recollect."

"Be there about the middle of the afternoon if everything goes right," the marshal replied.

Those calculations were correct, also. Around three o'clock they rode out of the hills and down into the cluster of trees and structures that made up the ancient settlement.

"Sure could use a drink," Metzgar said, wiping at his mouth with the back of a hand. "Bottle of mine went dry back up the trail a couple of days ago."

They had reached the edge of town and were riding up a narrow street that led to the plaza, around which were lined the stores and saloons. Abruptly Metzgar jerked his horse to a stop.

"There's Dixon!" he blurted in a strained voice. "Standing right there in front of that saloon! By God, I'll put an end to his deviling me right now!"

Thrusting his hand into a pocket of his coat, he drew out a nickel-plated revolver and leveled it at Gar Dixon.

"The hell you will!" Rye snarled and rocking to one side on his saddle he wrapped his fingers about the glinting weapon, and wrenched it from the jurist's grasp. "Shoot him and I'll have to take you in for murder!"

9

"How'd they know we'd come here?" Metzgar demanded, voice trembling with frustration. "You said they'd—"

"We'll talk about it later," Rye snapped, thrusting Metzgar's pistol, a small .32-caliber weapon, into a side pocket of his fringed jacket. "Best thing we can do is get the hell out of here before—"

"Too late," the jurist said as they wheeled their horses about. "Dixon's seen us. So has that brother-in-law of his."

Rye threw a hasty glance to the saloon. Gar Dixon, heavyset, tough-looking and matching the description given by Deputy Sheriff Charley Hoskins, had been joined by a second man—Saul Hillman, according to Metzgar.

But the lawman wasted no time in studying the two men who were now running toward the horses picketed at the side of the saloon. He had no desire to engage in a shootout with the two—not that he in any way feared the results of one; it was simply that he wanted to avoid any killing over Asa Metzgar. The Dixons and Saul Hillman were not outlaws, simply men with a vengeance fixation, and the best way to handle them, unless they actually got in the way, was to avoid them.

Cutting the chestnut about, and with Metzgar close by, he rushed back to the low-roofed adobe building at the upper end of the street, rounded it and spurred for its far end. Rye was thinking hard, trying to recall the exact layout of Socorro, searching his mind for the different routes that would lead east out of the settlement, lying at the northern edge of the infamous old trail from Mexico known as the *Jornado del Muerto*— the Journey of the Dead.

Reaching the corner of the structure he veered right. The street, little more than a narrow passageway between two adjacent buildings, should lead to the near end of the plaza, he figured. If so they could turn east and quickly make their way down to the river.

They came to a narrow cross alley, turned into it and followed along its narrow confines in single file until they reached another street. Rye halted, listened for sounds of Dixon and Hillman's horses coming up behind them. He could hear nothing. Moving into the street, he led the way down it and a few yards short of its end again stopped.

Dismounting, the lawman walked to the corner. To his right was the plaza. There was no sign of the two men, only of a half dozen loungers enjoying the shaded, grassy center of the plaza and three or four women moving along the sidewalk.

"Still would like to know how they knew we'd be here," Metzgar said.

Rye glanced over his shoulder. He thought the judge was still in his saddle. "Luck, I reckon. We went north, they went south around the mountains. Both ended up at the same place. And they could've figured we'd be headed here to stock up on grub."

"We should've figured this would happen and gone somewheres else," Metzgar grumbled. "Socorro can't be the only town with a general store in this part of the territory . . . Like to have my pistol back."

Rye considered for a long breath and then, taking the small Smith & Wesson from his pocket, handed it to Metzgar.

"Didn't know you carried a gun," he said, watching the judge slide the weapon into some sort of holster sewn inside his coat pocket.

"Man's got a right to protect himself—"

"And get himself killed if he doesn't know what he's doing," Rye snapped. "You keep that thing where it is. I'll do whatever shooting is necessary."

Metzgar made no reply as he stared out into the plaza. Then, "You see anything of Dixon and Hillman?"

Rye shook his head. "Nothing—and that bothers me, not knowing where they are. Wondering about the son, too. Where's he? Wasn't with them."

"He won't be far—probably in that saloon," Metzgar said. "We just going to keep standing here?"

"You are," Rye said abruptly, his voice sharp with anger and impatience. "Get back on your horse and stay here, out of sight."

"What're you going to do?"

"Dixon and Hillman just rode back into the plaza. Must have thought we went west; they came in from that direction."

"So?"

"I aim to put a stop to them dogging our tracks," Rye said. "Tired of watching out for them . . . Don't move from here."

Immediately Rye dropped back to where his horse waited and, mounting, rode out from between the two buildings, rounded the corner. Circling the plaza, the lawman headed slowly for the saloon, where Gar Dixon and Hillman were tying up their horses.

Ignoring the glances of the loafers in the parklike center of the square, and others along the sidewalk, the marshal continued on to where the two men, involved in conversation, were standing. A robin was singing in one of the nearby trees and a dozen sparrows were sporting about in the loose dust in front of a nearby livery stable.

Rye, taking in the surroundings, wished he knew where Devon Dixon was. It seemed illogical that he would still be in the saloon after his father and uncle had appeared on the street. But Rye could do nothing about that; he could only hope the younger Dixon wouldn't suddenly appear and complicate the situation. Whether Devon knew him or not Rye had no way of knowing, but it was certain that Gar and Saul Hillman were now aware of his presence, even if they didn't exactly know his identity.

Holding the chestnut to a slow walk, Rye drew near the saloon. He was slouched in the saddle, reins in his left hand, right one resting lightly on the butt of the .45 strapped to his hip. Suddenly Gar Dixon turned. Surprise flooded his ruddy face.

"There he is; that's him!" he yelled and made a stab for his own weapon.

"Don't!" Rye warned. "I'll kill you before you can clear leather!"

Dixon froze. Hillman, also reaching for the weapon he carried, paused, and following Dixon's example, raised his arms. Rye, gun now in hand, came off his horse slowly. Eyes still searching for the younger Dixon, he moved in quietly, to where the two men stood.

A crowd of both men and women had begun to gather, some looking on silently, others talking excitedly, and once Rye heard the words "Doomsday Marshal" as someone in the gathering recognized him.

"You've maybe got the drop on me now, but this ain't the last verse of this song," Dixon said in a low, tight voice. "I aim to kill that murdering sonofabitchin' judge—if I have to follow him—and you—clean to hell!"

"What's the trouble here?" a voice, coming from off to his left, demanded.

Rye did not turn. It would be the town marshal or someone from the sheriff's office, whichever represented the law in Socorro. He had noticed the man, star glinting on his vest, standing in front of one of the stores as he was closing in on Dixon and Hillman.

"What is it? What's going on?"

The lawman's voice was harsh as he moved up to where Rye could see him. A tall, lank man with dark features and coal-black eyes, he spoke with a slight accent. He was either Spanish or Mexican.

"I am a United States marshal, Sheriff," Rye said, reading the lawman's star. "I'm asking you to lock up these two men."

The sheriff frowned. His eyes narrowed suspiciously. "Sure, whatever you say. First off I want to see some identification."

Rye reached into a pocket and drew out the leather folder containing his papers and handed it to the sheriff without ever removing his gaze from Gar Dixon and Hillman. Back in the crowd, which was steadily growing larger, someone said gleefully: "See, I told you he was that marshal!"

The doubtful attitude of the sheriff vanished. He

handed the wallet back to Rye and said: "Sure, Marshal, glad to accommodate you," and then, he turned and beckoned to a younger man waiting off to one side, shotgun hanging in crook of an arm. Evidently a deputy and his backup.

"Henry, come get these two and throw them in a cell," he directed, relieving Dixon and Hillman of their weapons.

At once the deputy hurried forward and, with both hammers of the short-barreled shotgun at full cock, herded the two men off to the jail.

"Name's Herb Eagleton, Marshal," the sheriff said, extending his hand. "Glad to have you in my town— but I'll be needing charges to hold them."

"Interfering with the law," Rye said, glancing about for the younger Dixon. The crowd had begun to disperse but nowhere along the street did he see any sign of Devon Dixon.

"I've got an important, well, let's call him a prisoner that I'm taking east. That pair, and a son of one of them, have been dogging me since right out of Prescott, Arizona. They aim to take him away from me and kill him."

"Who is he?" Eagleton asked, turning to watch the deputy as he marched the two men toward the jail at the far end of a side street.

"Can't say, Sheriff. Just take my word for it he's important . . . Dixon's son is around here somewhere."

"Dixon; that their name?"

"The heavyset one is Gar Dixon. Man with him is a relative named Saul Hillman. Dixon's boy is called Devon."

"Don't sound familiar."

"Arizona people."

Eagleton rubbed at his jaw. "Not much of a charge to hold them on. How long you want me to keep them?"

"Till morning will do. That'll give me time to get my man pretty far up the road."

"I see. Which way you heading?"

Rye gave that brief consideration. He had no reason not to trust the lawman but such information did accidentally leak out at times.

"East—"

"For Texas."

Rye made no answer. Let Eagleton assume what he wished. It was better that way, but in truth they would be riding north, following the Rio Grande.

"I'm obliged to you, Sheriff," he said, extending his hand and turning for his horse. "Keeping that pair locked up overnight will be a big favor—'specially if you can pick up the son and hold him, too."

"Me and Henry'll start looking for him right away . . . Pleased to have met you, Marshal."

"Goes for me too, Sheriff . . . There a general store between here and the river?"

"Sure is—Dave Watson's. About halfway down the road."

Rye nodded and swung up into the saddle. The deputy, with his two prisoners, had evidently reached the jail as they were no longer to be seen, he noted as he cut about. Circling the plaza under the curious eyes of several bystanders, he returned to where Asa Metzgar was waiting.

"Let's move out," he said as he drew abreast the jurist.

Metzgar hesitated as if fearing to show himself and

then, as the lawman continued on down the street, hurriedly rode out of the shadow of the building where he'd been sitting on his horse and fell in beside the marshal.

"What happened? What about the Dixons?"

"They're in jail," Rye answered. "Be there until morning."

Metzgar heaved a deep sigh. "Guess that means we've seen the last of them."

John Rye was looking ahead at a fairly large building on their left. It would be Dave Watson's general store, he reckoned. He'd buy what they needed in grub and hurry on. With Devon Dixon on the loose he wasn't all that sure they had seen the last of the Dixon family.

10

"You get me a bottle?" Metzgar asked when Rye, grub sack refilled, stepped up into the saddle.

"No," the lawman replied, pulling away from the store's hitch rack and continuing on toward the river flowing sluggish and shallow between its banks.

"Why the hell not? Told you I was out of whiskey and needed—"

"Place don't carry liquor," Rye said, patience waning.

"Don't carry liquor!" the judge echoed. "What kind of a Holy Joe outfit is it?"

"Some stores carry a stock of liquor, some don't. Happens Watson's don't."

Metzgar muttered something under his breath as he shifted angrily on his saddle. "Well, how far's it going to be to where I can buy a bottle?"

"Couple of days. There's a town at the foot of those mountains on ahead. Be the only place."

The judge swore, scrubbed agitatedly at his jaw. After a bit he shrugged. "Expect I'll just have to hold out till then."

"Yeh, reckon you will," the marshal said dryly.

They reached the river, dropped south a quarter mile to the ford and crossed over. Gaining the east bank, Rye paused and, taking out his telescope, swept the road down which they had just come with a thorough scrutiny. There were several riders and a wagon on the south road that led to El Paso and the border. None of the men on horseback looked familiar.

"What're you looking for?" Metzgar demanded testily. "If you got the Dixons locked up like you claim there's no need for us to be watching out for them."

"Gar and Hillman are the ones in jail. I don't know if the sheriff ever found Devon or not. He and the deputy were going to try and run him down."

Rye put the telescope back into his saddlebags and raked the chestnut lightly with his spurs. While it would seem he had gotten the Dixons out of the picture insofar as their following him and the judge was concerned, he was still cautious and, ignoring the well-traveled road that ran northward along the river, he chose to stay on the trail where, shielded by the thick willows, wild olives and cottonwoods, their passage would be less noticeable.

Traveling along the quietly flowing Rio Grande would have been most pleasant had it been under different circumstances. The late-afternoon sun was warm, the soothing purl of the water was a balm to his nerves—turned a bit ragged by Metzgar's constant complaining—and the lack of other pilgrims on the trail was reassuring.

Meadowlarks whistled cheerfully from the fields that lay along both sides of the river, their presence being something he always remembered about the area. Ducks and geese could be seen flying both up and down the stream, wide at that point; cottontail rabbits scurried out of the low growth ahead of the horses, and once they frightened an old brindle Longhorn steer out of a patch of brush.

"You like this country?" Metzgar asked later, when near dark they halted for night camp.

Rye nodded. "Always found passing through it pleasant."

"Got mighty tired of it myself," the jurist replied. "Would have preferred to stay in the big towns altogether, but they kept me moving around."

Rye, unloading the packhorse, shrugged. "Can understand that."

"What do you mean by that?" Metzgar demanded instantly. "You saying it was because of the way I run my court?"

"Yeh, reckon I am—"

"Hell!" Metzgar said angrily, moving up to take the reins of the horses and the short lead rope affixed to the pack animal's halter, "I didn't have a choice. Was necessary. You've had to kill men; no difference in what I had to do."

"Some," Rye said mildly, unwilling to renew a subject they had already thrashed out. Making a point with the judge on the difference there was in the way each of them did their job was about as successful as dipping water from a creek with a fork.

"Never can seem to make you understand that I did only what was expected of me. Men I hung had it coming to them."

"Can say the same about the ones I had to shoot," Rye said. "They brought it on themselves, and doing that they cut down the odds on me killing an innocent man. Left no doubt they were guilty."

Metzgar shook his head in a gesture of frustration and moved off toward a small, narrow backwater from the river to picket the horses.

"Take the saddles off," Rye called as he began to prepare supper. "They'll need graining, too."

Metzgar had, surprisingly, assumed the chore of

looking after the horses during the long journey from
Clear Springs to Socorro.

"I don't need telling," he shot back and went on
about the task.

A short time later Rye had the meal ready and,
squatting by the fire, they both ate. When it was over
the lawman rinsed his plate and cup as well as the
frying pan and kettle in which he'd prepared
presoaked beans and salt pork, leaving the judge to
look after his own utensils.

An hour later they were in their blankets and under
their tarps, sleeping soundly. Shortly before first light
both awakened, and after a quick breakfast of bacon
and eggs—two of Rye's purchases at Watson's store—
they loaded up and were again in the saddle heading
north.

"That town you mentioned—"

"Apache Rocks—"

"Yes; will we get there before dark?" the judge
asked, lighting his pipe.

"Expect so, if we don't run into bad luck," the
lawman replied.

"Bad luck? You mean the Dixons?"

"Not so much them. I've been watching our back
trail and nobody's following us."

"Then what?"

"Rough country ahead. One of the horses could fall,
break a leg, or we could run into a party of Comanche-
ros. Been some seen around here lately."

A frown knotted Asa Metzgar's face. "This far north
of Mexico?"

"Not so much that as us being west of the
Chupadero Badlands. They've been seen there. And
we're in Mescalero Apache country."

"We're at peace with them," Metzgar said in a doubtful way. "Kit Carson rounded them up and put them on a reservation years ago. I don't think we have anything to fear from them."

"Not as a tribe, but there's always a few renegade parties looking to catch a lone pilgrim or two on the trail and rob them of all they've got."

Metzgar gave that thought for a time. Then, as the horses plodded steadily on over the uneven ground, he said, "You talk like you've put in a lot of time in this part of the country. Had it in mind that you worked more up Kansas way."

"Go wherever they send me," Rye answered. "Been from the Missouri west to the ocean—and from the Dakota and Montana borders right down to Mexico. Not much of the land in between that I haven't seen— some parts more than others."

"Expect that means you don't have a family—"

Rye was silent for a time and then shrugged. "No, not any more," he said in a way that said the subject was closed.

"I've been wondering," Metzgar said thoughtfully, "if you're like most of the men I've come up against out here; you running away from something, too?"

John Rye considered that for several moments, eyes on several vultures lazily circling high above the hills.

"Maybe only from myself," he said, "and the past."

"Well, whatever it is," the judge said, "you'll never get away from it. You'll always find it running right alongside of you."

The marshal's gaze was now straight ahead, seemingly fixed on the increasingly broken land they were entering as they drew nearer the mountains. Long ago he had come to terms with himself, convinced that he'd never entirely free his mind from the past, of the memory of the days in faraway St. Louis and the woman he had loved—and neglected. There was no going back in time to rectify the mistakes he'd made then; he simply had to live with it.

"Expect so," he said, more to quiet the judge and put an end to the painful topic.

"See smoke ahead," Metzgar remarked after a time. "That the town you're talking about—Apache Rocks?"

"That'll be it."

"Sure be glad to get there," Metzgar said with a long sigh. "You think we could stay there overnight, have a decent meal in a restaurant and sleep in a bed?"

"No reason why not," Rye said and, prompted by the smell of Metzgar's tobacco smoke, took a cigar from his case and lit up. "We're coming in early, and long as there's nobody on our trail, I'm all for it."

11

They reached the end of the road leading into Apache Rocks, a small collection of houses, two saloons, a general store and a combination hotel and restaurant crouched at the base of a slate-gray cliff. Rye halted and, drawing the telescope from its place in his weather-bleached saddlebags, leveled it on the country they had just covered and searched it minutely. He could see no riders, no movement of any kind in fact, and, restoring the glass to its customary carrying place, nodded to Metzgar.

"Nobody in sight. Be no reason why we can't spend the night here."

Metzgar smiled. "Was afraid you might change your mind about it," he said, relief in his voice. "I'll be obliged if you'll take care of the horses this time, and see to getting us a room. I've got to get a drink."

Rye's solid-looking shoulders stirred. Stabling the horses was Metzgar's job, but he had become accustomed to the jurist shirking camp chores and thought little of the request. Too, he reckoned the judge was suffering from his lack of whiskey, a palliative no doubt to ease his conscience.

"Go ahead, I'll meet you in that saloon after I'm done," he said, jerking a thumb at a building bearing a faded sign above its doorway that labeled it "The Sunnyside."

Metzgar immediately dropped from his saddle and

walked rapidly toward the saloon. Rye watched the jurist for a few moments and then, reaching out, took up the reins of Metzgar's bay and continued on for the hotel, a low-roofed, rock-walled affair of perhaps a half dozen rooms.

Glancing beyond he saw the livery stable, set well to the rear. It was also of rock and, veering away from the hostelry's hitch rack that fronted the inn, he moved on to the lesser structure. The door was open and, riding in leading Metzgar's bay, and with the little packhorse close by, he halted. He could hear voices coming from a small office off to his left.

Abruptly the conversation ceased and a squat, bearded man in overalls appeared in the doorway. He nodded genially. "Howdy, friend, what can I do for you?"

"Want these horses looked after," Rye answered.

"Sure enough. You putting up for the night at the hotel?" the hostler said, stepping down into the runway and grasping the chestnut's bridle.

"We are," the lawman said as he dismounted. "Be riding out first thing in the morning."

"They'll be ready," the stableman said, looking over the horses and the gear. "You be wanting any of this stuff?"

Rye drew the shotgun from its scabbard and hung it in the crook of an arm and then, taking his saddlebags, started for the door.

"If my friend wants anything from his horse he'll be in after it himself."

The hotel had no customers and the choice of rooms was his, the owner of the establishment advised Rye as he signed the dog-eared register. The lawman reckoned it didn't really matter where they slept and left it up to the hotel man, who obliged by putting them in the best room the place had to offer—on the south side and in the rear.

Depositing his gear, Rye, somewhat ill at ease at the thought of Asa Metzgar out of sight, left the hotel and made his way to the Sunnyside Saloon. Entering the open doorway he spotted the judge sitting alone at a table in the back of the room. He had a bottle and two glasses before him and when he saw the marshal, he half rose and beckoned vigorously.

"Was beginning to think you weren't coming," Metzgar said as Rye settled on a chair. "Was getting a mite lonesome. Folks around here aren't the friendliest I've ever come across . . . We all set for the night?" he added, pouring the lawman a drink.

"All set," Rye replied, tossing off the liquor and glancing about.

The saloon was little more than an ordinary-sized room graced by a counter at one end and a cluster of tables and chairs in its center. The rough, unfinished lumber sides were bare and the only source of light after darkness fell appeared to be several lamps in brackets affixed to the walls. There was no mirrored backbar, only three shelves sagging under the weight of bottles and glasses.

"Man could call this place a dump," Metzgar commented, watching Rye closely as the lawman took stock of the place. "Whiskey's good, however. Not the usual rotgut you'd expect to get."

Rye nodded agreement, poured himself another drink and resumed his contemplation of the Sunnyside. Other than the bartender, who likely was also the owner—an average-sized, balding man in dark shirt and pants, there were six other patrons present, two at one table, four at another. The latter were engaged in a game of cards; the pair, however, slouched sullenly in their chairs doing nothing but take turn at their bottle.

After a bit the bartender, time hanging heaving on his hands, forsook the counter and crossed to where Rye and Metzgar sat.

"First time I've seen you gents in my place; I'm Ben Hudkins. Sure want to make you feel welcome."

Rye nodded. Metzgar smiled and said: "We're just passing through. Want to compliment you on the brand of whiskey you sell."

"Best I can buy," Hudkins said with pride. "I got men who ride in here from as far as fifty miles to do their drinking. You both look like you've been forking a saddle for quite a spell."

"Going on two weeks," Metzgar said. "Still got two or three more ahead of us."

Rye frowned. Liquor was loosening Metzgar's tongue. He caught the jurist's eye, shook his head warningly.

"Mighty long time to be riding. Where you going?" the barman asked.

"Nebraska—my hometown, Plattesville," Metzgar said promptly.

Rye swore under his breath. Hudkins shifted his attention to the lawman.

"That your hometown, too?"

"No, he's from a little bit of everywhere," Metzgar answered before the lawman could reply. "He's John Rye, a U.S. marshal—the one they call the Doomsday Marshal. He's just riding along with me."

Hudkins' eyes widened in surprise. "You him?" he

said in an incredulous voice. "I sure never expected to—"

Rye angry, patience at an end, got to his feet. "Come on, Asa, we'd best be going," he said, taking the judge by the arm and pulling him to his feet. "Let's eat."

"You staying the night?" Hudkins asked, apparently hopeful of capitalizing on the presence of the famed lawman.

Rye nodded. "The hotel the best place to get some supper?"

"The only one," the saloonkeeper said, "unless you're willing to settle for some stew I've got on the stove in the back room."

"Obliged to you, but we're needing a full meal. Come on, Judge, let's go—"

Metzgar, unsteady on his feet, corked his bottle of liquor and took it by the neck. "I paid you for this, didn't I, bartender?"

"You sure did," Hudkins said, smiling. "Now, come on back after dark. Place gets a bit more lively then, and if you're hankering for a little female company there's some ladies down the road who usually show up looking for a good time."

"We'll keep it in mind," Rye said, taking a firmer grip on Metzgar's arm and starting for the door.

At that moment the saloon's entrance darkened as a tall, broad-shouldered man in rancher's clothing paused briefly in the opening and then entered.

"Howdy there, Jake," Hudkins greeted as he moved back behind the bar. "Wasn't expecting you till later."

"Got an early start," Jake said. He came to an abrupt halt, a frown tearing at his forehead as he stared at Metzgar. Suddenly he dropped back a step.

"You're Metzgar—that goddamn Hanging Judge!" he shouted and made a stab for the gun on his hip.

Rye drew fast, fired, taking no particular aim. The bullet struck the man in the left forearm, spun him half around as the room boomed with the echo of the shot and layers of smoke began to hover about Rye and Metzgar.

The lawman threw a narrow, warning glance at the other men in the room, now on their feet and edging toward him and Metzgar. As they came to a stop, he stepped forward to where Jake was gripping his bleeding arm. Jerking the rancher's pistol from its holster, he dropped back.

"Who the hell are you?" he heard Jake mutter.

"I'm the law," Rye replied and slid a look at Metzgar. "Know him?"

"Recognize him now," the judge answered, all whiskey-induced thickness gone from his voice. "Name's Jake Bedford. I—"

"You hung my brother—a year ago in Arkansas," Bedford said in a low, tense way. "He never done what you had him strung up for. Proved that later, but, god damn you, you wouldn't wait for us to do it!"

"Your brother got a fair trial—"

"He got tried, all right, but there sure wasn't nothing fair about it. Even that shyster you had working with you was willing to hold off till the boys from that cattle drive got back and could tell you Abe wasn't guilty. But no, you, in your almighty hurry to string Abe up, wouldn't listen to nobody; you just went ahead and—and murdered him for something he didn't do!"

Bedford's voice had risen to a higher pitch and he

was trembling with anger. "Swore right then and there that if I ever seen you again I'd kill you!"

"Forget it, Bedford," Rye said sternly. "It's all over and done with."

"Who the hell are you?"

"Told you once. I'm a U.S. marshal. Metzgar's under my protection."

"Means nothing to me—and no U.S. marshal's going to keep me from—"

"Back off, Jake," one of the four men who had been sitting at a table broke in as he moved up beside Bedford. "The law's looking out for this man—"

"He ain't no man; he's a hanging judge!" Bedford shouted.

The smoke that had bulged up about Rye and Metzgar had drifted away but the smell of burnt gunpowder still hung in the air.

"Better listen to your friend, Bedford," Rye said quietly. "You don't want trouble with me."

The rancher, awkwardly wrapping a red bandanna taken from his pants pocket about the wound in his arm, shook his head. "Trouble don't mean nothing to me; I been living on it all my life."

"Which will end right here if you give me any more problems," Rye said curtly and, tossing Bedford's pistol to Hudkins, added: "Don't give that gun back to him until he cools off. Understand?"

"Yes, sir, Marshal," the bartender said. "Me and the rest of his friends'll keep him right here till he settles down."

There apparently was no lawman or jail in Apache Rocks, Rye decided, so he could not have Jake Bedford jailed for safekeeping as he had the Dixons, but he felt reasonably sure Hudkins and the others would keep the man under control—not that he would rely fully on the probability. He'd have to keep an eye open for Bedford all the time they would be in Apache Rocks, and likely, if he was to put any stock in Jake Bedford's words, for a while after they departed.

"Move!" he said sharply to Metzgar and immediately began to hurry the judge past the rancher and the hard-eyed men looking on.

The possibility that he just might not get Asa Metzgar back to his home in Nebraska alive had never entered Rye's mind, but now a thread of doubt was rising. How many more Dixons and Bedfords, all bent on killing the man, would they encounter before reaching Nebraska? He was aware that Asa Metzgar had made a host of enemies, but he hadn't realized there could be so much violent hatred calling for the death of the man.

Passing through the doorway and out into the fading sunlight, the lawman released his grip on Metzgar's arm, and turned toward the hotel. The incident in the saloon had sobered the judge considerably and he now spoke in a serious vein and with a clear mind.

"That man's a lunatic!" he declared. "His brother killed a man. There was no doubt."

Rye smiled tightly. "You'll sure as hell never convince him of that . . . Let's eat and turn in. I want to ride out by first light."

"You think it's safe to spend the night here?"

Rye shook his head, spat into the dust. "I'm hoping so. The horses need the rest, same as we can use a good night's sleep."

"I agree with that," Metzgar said, "but if Bedford comes after us with a gun in his hand will you kill him?"

"If I have to—"

Metzgar turned his small dark eyes on the marshal. There was a half smile on his thin lips. "I guess there's not much difference in us after all," he drawled. "You do what you have to do—same as I did."

12

"I'll take my gun back, Sheriff. So'll my partner," Gar Dixon said coldly.

Herb Eagleton, sitting at his desk, glanced up as Deputy Henry Stokes led the two men into his office. He reckoned there was nothing he could do but comply with Dixon's demand. He'd held the pair overnight as John Rye had requested, thus allowing the marshal and the man he had in custody to be well on their way by that hour. Too, he'd actually had no real charge to jail Dixon and Hillman on.

Without comment, Eagleton opened the lower drawer of his desk and, producing the two belted pistols, laid them out before the two men.

"Aim to give you a little advice," the lawman said.

Dixon, in the act of strapping on his gun belt, hawked, spat on the floor. "Keep it!" he snarled. "I don't need nothing from you."

"You're going to get it anyway," Eagleton shot back, coming to his feet. "That lawman you're fooling with is John Rye—the one they call the Doomsday Marshal. Just realized that last night when I was looking through some papers."

"What the hell's the Doomsday Marshal?" Hillman asked.

"He's the man who'll kill you quicker than you can bat an eye if you cross him. Don't know what you've got in mind, but you sure'n hell better stay clear of him."

Gar Dixon, six-gun in place on his hip, glanced at Hillman. Neither man had shaved in days and the bristly beard each now wore gave them a look of fierceness.

"I reckon we know what we're doing, don't we, Saul," he said and, pivoting on a heel, crossed to the doorway and out into the early-morning sunshine. After a few strides Hillman caught up with him.

"Maybe we best listen to that sheriff, Gar, and forget what we're aiming to do," he said. "Could be we're biting off more'n we can chew."

Dixon halted, shook his head angrily. Farther on a ways he could see his son, Devon, approaching with their horses. He'd wondered what had happened to the boy, was relieved to see that he was all right. Abruptly he wheeled to Hillman.

"Hell with that. Ain't no lawdog going to keep me from squaring up with that killing judge. Now, if you're getting cold feet, why, you just climb on your horse and head on back home. Me and Devon ain't quitting till we've settled with Metzgar."

Hillman stared off in the direction of the misty gray mountains far to the east. "I ain't getting cold feet; you know me better'n that, Gar," he said quietly. "I'm only wanting us to be sensible about this. Getting ourselves killed by that marshal ain't going to bring back Cord and Price."

"Maybe not," Dixon said, shifting his attention back to Devon and the horses now halting before him, "but we'll have evened things up for them if we ain't killed . . . Where you been, boy?" he added as his eldest son dismounted.

"Hiding out mostly," Devon replied. "That sheriff and his deputy was hunting me. I reckon they was going to lock me up, too."

"Just what they had in mind."

"Well, I didn't stay hid out. Was having me a drink with a gal I met in the saloon—up in her room. When I seen that jasper and the judge—"

"That jasper's a U.S. marshal—one of the hard-case ones," Hillman cut in.

Devon let that register and shrugged. "Anyway, when I seen them leaving after you got hauled off to the hoosegow by that deputy, I sort of followed—figuring we ought to know where they was going. They went straight down to the river."

"You for sure they didn't spot you spying on them?" Gar asked.

"Made dang sure. Was a family in a wagon on the same road heading for someplace called San Antonio; it's somewhere south of Socorro. I just made myself one of their party, rode right alongside them for a bit, then cut back. If this here lawdog, whatever his name is, was watching, he'd a thought I was with them folks. What's that marshal's name, anyway?"

"John Rye, the sheriff said," Hillman answered. "Got a real tough reputation, according to the sheriff. Folks have nicknamed him the Doomsday Marshal."

"Sounds real mean—"

"The kind that don't mind killing. Told your pa that maybe we ought to give up on Metzgar, go on back home."

Devon turned to his parent. A wagon wheeled past nearby, setting up a cloud of dust that momentarily drifted over them.

"What's that you say, Pa?"

"That lawdog don't mean nothing. Pulls on his pants same way I do," Gar responded. "Far as quitting and going home, told Saul he could pull out anytime, that you and me ain't backing off till that hanging judge was dead."

Devon nodded. "Sure just how I feel, too."

"Figured you would. Now, you say you followed the marshal and Metzgar down to the river? Which way did they go after they got there?"

"Headed north—upriver."

"North," Gar repeated thoughtfully. "Had it in mind they'd point for Texas. Where the hell you reckon they're going heading that way?"

It was a rhetorical question voiced at low breath by Gar Dixon, and one to which he never expected an answer.

"They've got a long start on us," Hillman said. "If we're aiming to keep after them we best get moving."

"They ain't likely to be far ahead," Dixon said, taking the reins of his horse from his son and swinging up into the saddle. "They got to sleep and eat too."

"Seen them pull up at a general store when they was about halfway down to the river," Devon said and mounted his horse, a white-faced bay. "Expect they was buying grub."

"Something we best do, too. We're running short on about everything," Hillman said, also climbing onto his horse.

"All right, we'll stop there and get what we have to have," Gar said. "Got to go easy on the buying, howsomever. I'm starting to run short of cash."

"Maybe that counterjumper at the store can tell us where the marshal and the judge were heading,"

Devon said as they began to turn toward the plaza and the road leading down to the Rio Grande.

"He just might at that," Gar agreed, glancing in the direction of the jail. The sheriff and his deputy were standing in front of the doorway watching them. "You still for certain they rode north? Could've made it look like that for a piece, then cut right for Texas."

"They didn't long as I kept them in sight—and that was for quite a spell," Devon stated flatly. "If they done like you say, they did it a far piece up the river."

"Misdoubt that. They would've headed for the main road east right off, so's not to lose a lot of time."

Gar paused, glanced upward. They were facing a sun that was climbing steadily into a pure blue sky, and its heat was already making itself felt. A flock of ducks was winging its way down the river, their dark shapes like fast-moving arrowheads in the morning light. A dog barked from somewhere in the distance, and for a moment Gar Dixon wished he were back home tending his ranch and cattle and things were as they had been before his sons Cord and Price got into trouble. But that could never be; they were dead—thanks to Asa Metzgar.

"We'll all go in," he said as they swung onto the hard-pack fronting Watson's store and halted at the hitch rack. "Saul, you do the buying. I'll talk to the counterjumper sort of offhand, see what I can find out."

Picketing the horses, they marched up the steps, crossed the landing and, opening the dust-clogged screen door, entered. The storekeeper, wiping his hands on his flour-sack apron, came forward to meet them.

"Morning, gentlemen. What can I do for you?"

"You Watson?" Gar asked in a friendly tone.

"Sure am—"

"Well, we're needing some grub. My partner there's got a list in his head. You take care of him while me and my boy have a look around."

"Sure thing," the storekeeper said and put his attention on Saul Hillman. "Go right ahead, mister, start calling off your list."

Hillman began to name the items they would be needing as the merchant scribbled the order on a piece of paper. When he had finished and had started collecting the articles, Gar paused nearby.

"Looking for a couple of friends," he said. "Figured we might run into them around here."

Watson looked up. "Could've been the pair that was here early this morning. One was an old-like man, other was younger. Heard his friend call him Shorty."

"Wouldn't've been them. Men we're looking for likely was here yesterday afternoon—late."

Watson continued to fill Hillman's order, a deep frown on his clean-shaven features. Suddenly he smiled. "Yeh, I remember now. They came by here late in the day. One stayed in the saddle, the other one bought some groceries, the trail-grub kind."

"Probably them all right. One was wearing a fringed jacket—"

"He was the one who came in. Sort of a soft-spoken man, but all business."

"Them for sure," Gar Dixon said. "He happen to mention where they were headed? We've all been talking about going to Texas."

Watson shook his head as he finished assembling the order Hillman had given him. "Nope, never said anything about that. He was sort of a closemouthed man. Acted like he had something against talking."

Gar shrugged in frustration. Why the hell couldn't that damn lawdog have dropped at least a hint as to where he and Metzgar were headed? Nothing ever came easy. Seemed everything always had to be the hard way. Coming about, he glanced at Hillman, who was digging into his pocket for money to pay for the purchases.

"Ain't no need for that, Saul," he said, producing several silver dollars and handing them to his brother-in-law. "Pay the man off and let's get moving."

13

There was no sign of Jake Bedford when Rye and Asa Metzgar mounted up and rode out of Apache Rocks that next morning. Nor had they heard from the rancher during the night. Evidently his friends had done a good job of keeping the man settled down, hopefully for good. But Rye was not counting on it; when they reached a high rise north of the settlement a time later, he drew to a halt and looked back.

The sun had just cleared the mountainous horizon to the east and the land, all green grass, giant cottonwood and other, lesser trees, grayish shrubbery and the silver ribbon of the Rio Grande cutting through it all along the floor of the valley appeared fresh and new.

"You see anybody coming?" Metzgar asked.

Rye, now taking out his telescope to search their back trail and seeing no one, shook his head. "Nobody in sight."

Metzgar swore. "Hell, Jake won't be giving up that easy. Could see it in his eyes; he's dead set on killing me. Why the devil didn't you put that bullet in him where it would do some good?"

Rye shrugged and put the glass away. "I'm not here to kill every man who comes along aiming to get even with you. My job's to see you make it home alive."

"Never do it the way you're going about it!" the judge said angrily as they moved on. "You'll have to use that gun of yours—not just to threaten or maybe wing somebody, but to cut them down. I'm beginning to wonder if all that talk about you being a killer marshal is only smoke."

Killer marshal. Rye smiled tightly at the term. It was on the same level as *Hanging Judge* and, as far as he was concerned, had the same taint to it.

"I'd like to think you're right," he said, glancing ahead.

They were drawing near a small settlement of some kind, and the fields off to their left were crowded with ripening corn, heavily laden chili plants, melons and beans. At once Rye cut to the right and headed up into a rougher, rock-strewn area.

"What're we doing this for?" Metzgar protested, hands gripping the horn of his saddle to keep from being thrown as his horse stumbled and almost went down. "Could've stayed down below where—"

"And be seen by the people in that town?" Rye said, pointing to the cluster of houses a half mile or so farther on. "Got to keep covering our trail."

"If you're thinking about Jake Bedford, he'll know we rode north—"

"Know that. I'm talking about the Dixons, and maybe the man who called himself Smith and his partner Shorty that I told you about. If they're following blind and get to Apache Rocks, they'll find out all they want to know."

"Don't see how."

"Easy. All that talking you did back there in Hudkins' saloon. You let the world know we were headed for Nebraska—something you sure as hell should've kept to yourself. Anybody looking to kill you won't even need to follow us if they aren't of a mind; can just work ahead and be waiting somewhere."

"Big country," Metzgar said indifferently. "They can't watch all the trails and roads."

"Common sense will tell them that since we're headed in this direction, we'll follow the trail that cuts north across the Indian Territory panhandle."

Metzgar gave that thought, his gaze now on the distant village in the valley. Blue-gray smoke was trickling upward from three or four sources, and the far-off, hollow sound of someone chopping wood was a lonely sound in the still, cool air.

"Could take a different road—"

"No, our best chance is the shortest one—the way we're going now," Rye snapped.

He was in poor humor, the remembrance of the carelessness Metzgar had displayed back in the Apache Rocks saloon galling him. All the pains he'd taken to keep secret the route they would be taking, as well as their ultimate destination, had been nullified by Metzgar's loose talk. But the damage was done. There was little he could do about it now except try to keep out of sight and hope, somehow, to beat the Dixons and anyone else following them to Nebraska.

Metzgar remained silent for a long time as the horses picked their way up the gradually ascending trail that wound its way through rock, scrub oak, piñon and other minor growth, but finally he broke his stillness.

"You said something about a John Smith and a Shorty somebody. I don't recollect ever knowing either one."

"Caught them trailing me out of Prescott. They claimed they were just heading in the same direction, but from the way they acted I'm pretty sure they were lying."

"That name—John Smith—sounds kind of bogus to me. What did he look like?"

"Forty years old or thereabouts. Tall, lean man. Was wearing denim pants, black leather vest. Boots looked like he'd been working cattle in brush country. I remember he was wearing a narrow-brimmed brown hat—the kind you usually see in town."

Metzgar stroked his chin thoughtfully for a bit and then shook his head. "Sure don't remember anybody fitting that description coming up before me; but there's been so many. What did his partner look like?"

"Short, small man. Was younger. Couldn't see him very good. I'd say he was a working cowhand. Called himself Shorty Pedgett."

"Don't know him either."

Rye stirred. "Could be they were who and what they claimed and have got nothing to do with you."

The lawman studied the trail ahead. It was becoming steeper and that fact was causing the horses to slow. They were beginning to lose time, and if there was anyone following them—and Rye was certain there was—slowing down wasn't a very reassuring thought.

"We going to be making camp soon?" the judge asked after a time. "Sure getting tired."

"Be a while yet," the lawman replied.

He glanced back over his shoulder. Directly behind him was the bay packhorse following close on the heels of the chestnut, as always. A short distance farther on was Asa Metzgar, and beyond him the trail they had just covered. Rye studied it minutely. As far as he could see there were no other riders. Taking satisfaction in that, he returned his attention to the horse the judge was riding. It appeared to have a limp.

"Your horse going lame?" he called.

Metzgar pulled to a stop instantly. Rye cut his chestnut about and dropped back. Metzgar was already off the saddle, looking down at the bay's hooves.

"Which foot? Sure hope there's nothing wrong—"

Rye dismounted and crossed to the judge's horse and, bending down, tapped the bay's left foreleg. The horse raised his hoof at once. The marshal swore. The shoe was almost worn completely away, leaving only the inner side—and it was loose. Releasing the bay's leg, he examined the remaining shoes, found them all badly worn.

"You should have had this horse shod before we left Clear Springs!" Rye said, glancing angrily at the judge.

Metzgar nodded. "Thought about having a blacksmith look at them but the Dixons were around and I was afraid they'd spot me, so I put it off. You think the ones he's wearing will hold out till we get to the next town?"

"Be a couple of days before we reach one. I'll see if I can nail that left front shoe down tighter—and then hope it'll hold out till we get to Greasewood, the closest place. If it won't, you'll be in for some walking."

"The hell I will," Metzgar came back angrily. "I'll ride double with you."

"No," Rye said flatly. "Country's too hard on a horse carrying one man, and doubling his load is wrong. Like I said, I'll see what I can do about it tonight after we've made camp."

They made camp late that day in a coulee about halfway up a long slope. Following the usual routine they had lapsed into, Metzgar saw to the care of the horses and brought up a supply of firewood while Rye set up the camp and prepared the meals. The chore of being the cook didn't particularly please or displease the lawman, as he was accustomed to feeding himself while on the trail, and he accepted it as a matter of course; too, he doubted the ability of the judge, who had lived most of his life in towns and settlements where restaurant fare was available, to put together an edible meal.

Taking time while it was still daylight, Rye again examined the shoes on Metzgar's bay and succeeded in tightening them all by using a flat rock as a hammer. With luck the horse should be able to make it to Greasewood, the next town, without laming himself—if not pressed too hard.

That troubled John Rye, and he gave it considerable thought as he went about his camp duties. Jake Bedford, assuming he was following them, which was most likely, would not be far behind. And Gar Dixon, with his son and brother-in-law, most certainly would be somewhere in the area, actually on their trail also if the Socorro sheriff had not found and locked up the son.

Devon, if he had remained free, would have watched and seen Metzgar and him when they left the town and noted which direction they had taken once they had reached the river. And even if the younger Dixon had not thought to keep an eye on them, someone certainly would have seen them passing and relayed the information to the Dixons when asked. From that point on Gar and his party would have it easy; the judge's whiskey talk would see to that.

But there was no sign of any of them, including John Smith and Shorty Pedgett, that next morning when they rode out, and Rye, from one of the higher ridges, took special pains to search the country behind them with his glass. He felt some better when his careful examination of the trail revealed no riders. Maybe they were running in luck; perhaps they had managed somehow to throw Metzgar's vengeance seekers off their heels, but deep down inside, Rye considered that most improbable.

Still, that belief strengthened that following day, when around mid afternoon they halted at the edge of Greasewood and there was still no indication of their being pursued.

14

Jake Bedford awoke in the back room of Hudkins' Sunnyside Saloon. His mouth was dry and his eyes felt as if they were in the back of his throbbing head. It was dark and he could hear no sounds coming from the adjoining saloon area and, pulling himself to his feet, he stood for a long minute collecting his wavering senses and staring down at his bandaged forearm.

Slowly, it all came back to him. He had come face to face with Asa Metzgar, the Hanging Judge, the one man he hated most in all the world. He had reached for his gun, fully intending to kill Metzgar, but the man—a lawman—with the judge had drawn his six-gun and shot him in the arm.

Evidently Ben Hudkins had got his wife to take care of the wound, which really wasn't much, and then Hudkins and the rest of his friends in the saloon had managed to get enough liquor into him to keep him there—probably afraid the lawman who'd plugged him would do the job up permanent if they met again.

Well, by hell, it wasn't going to end there, Bedford thought grimly and started for the door. His mind had cleared now and there was no unsteadiness in his movements. He had been hoping for a chance to confront Asa Metzgar, who, in his estimation, was nothing more than a cheap murderer who got away with his killings simply because he was a judge—a hanging judge, Jake had heard the man called many times.

He'd settle with him for hanging Abe, his only brother, and with that lawman, too, who'd stuck his nose into something that was none of his butt-in.

Bedford reached the door and entered the deserted saloon. Several crickets were noisily breaking the hush as he crossed to the Sunnyside's entrance and, as he stepped out onto the landing fronting the saloon, a dog trotting along the dusty street began to bark at his unexpected appearance.

Ignoring the startled animal, Jake crossed to the rack at the corner of the building where he had left his horse. The sorrel was still there, slack-hipped and dozing. Evidently Hudkins and the others had expected him to wake up sooner and go home, otherwise one of them would have stabled the gelding in the barn back of the saloon.

Mounting up, paying no mind to the slight pain in his forearm, Bedford rode out of the settlement for what he was pleased to call his ranch, although most termed it a farm, some five miles east.

Anger was still simmering within him when he reached the scatter of four or five buildings that made up his holdings, and, going direct to the barn, he removed the gear for the sorrel he was riding and put it on a big gray. He'd need a strong horse, one with plenty of bottom, to do what he had in mind, and such called for the gray.

That done, Jake hung his saddlebags across his shoulder and started for the house. His arrival had awakened his wife, and she was standing in the kitchen doorway, a lamp in her hand, as he entered.

"I was beginning to worry," she said, and then broke

off when she saw the bandage on his arm. "You—you've been fighting again!"

"It's only a scratch, Annie," he said and, brushing on by her, went to the shelving on the wall and started filling his saddlebags with the items of food he would need, taking also a handful of currency and silver dollars out of the crock that served as a depository.

"What's wrong? Where are you going?" Annie asked anxiously. "Is the law after you?"

"No, I run into that damn judge that strung up Abe. Aim to settle with him."

A moan of anguish escaped the woman's thin lips. Her dull eyes took on a brightness and the lines of her worn face deepened.

"Oh, Jake—I thought you'd forgotten all that—that all that hate was behind you!"

"I ain't never forgetting none of it," Bedford said in a low, hard way, buckling the flaps of his saddlebags. "I'll never sleep good, long as that man's alive."

"Where is he? I thought you'd seen him here in town—but you're fixing to travel."

"He's close by—heading north with some lawman."

"Lawman!" Annie echoed in a falling voice.

"Yeh," Jake said, moving toward the door. "Looks like things got so hot for him that the government had to put a lawman to looking out for him."

"And that lawman'll probably kill you, Jake, if you go trying to shoot Metzgar. You best realize that."

"Reckon he can try; I ain't saying he can do it . . . Tell the boys to look out for things while I'm gone. I'll be back when you see me."

Annie nodded resignedly. "I expect I will," she said in a toneless voice and, following him to the door, listened briefly to the rap of his heels on the hard-pack as he crossed to his horse. Then, closing the thick iron-strapped panel, she turned and wearily made her way back to bed.

15

Greasewood was somewhat more than a small town, as towns in that sparsely settled part of New Mexico territory went. A dozen or more business houses, a quarter of which were saloons, stood along the single main street together with a hotel named Hilltop, a restaurant designated as Murphy's Best Eatery, Tom Evans' Livery Stable and the usual run of other firms.

Adjoining the stable was a small, narrow building that bore the sign "Stage Depot," which brought to John Rye's mind the just-remembered fact that he'd been told Greasewood was once an important stop for several stagecoaches. A new route had dimmed the settlement's importance as a crossroads hub for the coaches, and it was now served by a single line.

"Like to get myself another bottle—"

At Asa Metzgar's words Rye shifted his eyes to the nearest saloon—the Silver Spur. He shook his head.

"We'll swing in behind that first one—and I'll go in. Don't want you being seen any more than necessary."

"Hell!" Metzgar protested. "I was looking forward to a little company. You're not the best I've ever been around, you know."

"Tough," Rye said and, raking the chestnut lightly with his spurs, started him toward the alley that ran behind the structures on that side of the dusty roadway.

"What do you want me to do?"

"Go on to the hotel, sign in for both of us. Stay in the room till I get there. I'll see to the horses."

"You're aiming to spend the night here?"

"More or less have to. Horse of yours needs shoeing, and they all can use some rest," the lawman said as they drew in behind the saloon. "Was no sign of anybody on our trail. Just hoping it'll stay that way."

"Guess I'm a mite tired, too," Metzgar said as the lawman dismounted. "You know, Marshal, I can't figure you. It's been said you're a hard-case lawman, one that never backed down from using your gun, but here we are running like scared rabbits from this Dixon bunch, and maybe Jake Bedford—and those two others. Don't quite understand—"

"Not hard to figure it out," Rye said. "None of them are outlaws. They're all ordinary men that just happen to have a grudge stuck crosswise in their gullet. Maybe they've got a right—"

"Right!" Metzgar echoed angrily. "You standing up for them? Sounds like you're saying they've got a right to kill me!"

"No, not saying that at all. Fact is I've got no opinion on whether they're right or wrong because I plain don't know. My job's to—"

"Being a lawman you ought to take my side of it regardless of what they think, and shoot down any of them that tries to kill me."

"I figure it's better to not let them get close enough for that," Rye said and, crossing to the back door of the saloon, entered.

Returning a few minutes later with a quart bottle of whiskey, he handed it up to the jurist and swung back into the saddle of the weary chestnut.

"Hotel's on down the street, same side as this," he

said. "When you check us in, use some other name besides your real one."

"What about eating?" Metzgar asked as they moved off down the trash-littered alleyway.

"I'll have supper brought up to the room. Safer that way."

Metzgar had uncorked the bottle and was having himself a drink. He did not offer the whiskey to Rye, either out of neglect or under the assumption the marshal would turn it down.

"Expect you're right. We sure don't want to take any chances, no, sir!"

That was his intention, Rye agreed, ignoring the trace of sarcasm in Metzgar's words. He was hating the job of seeing Asa Metzgar safely to his Nebraska home more every day, and the task was correspondingly more difficult.

But he guessed he'd be able to get the job done if he kept his eyes open and didn't take any chances. He only hoped he could accomplish it without having to use his gun, as Metzgar wanted him to do, on the misguided men who were out seeking vengeance on the man they called the Hanging Judge.

The Dixons, Jake Bedford, John Smith and Shorty Pedgett could all be good men with a perfect right to what they thought about Metzgar, but he couldn't let that influence him. Metzgar had rights, too, and Rye was charged with seeing that those rights were protected and that the man reached his home alive.

They came to the hotel, so designated by a large spur painted on the door of the establishment. Leaving it up to the judge to carry in their gear and arrange for quarters, Rye continued on to the livery stable with the horses.

"The bay with the saddle on needs shoeing," the lawman told the hostler as he came up from the shadowy depths of the musky-smelling barn. "Where's the blacksmith?"

"We don't got one," the hostler, a small dark man of Spanish or Mexican descent, replied. "He is next door."

Rye nodded and, turning the chestnut and the packhorse over to the hostler to strip, began to remove the gear from Metzgar's bay. Without asking, he hung the saddle over the wall of the first stall and, leaving the bridle in place, turned to lead the judge's animal back to the street.

"You will want the horses in the morning?"

"Maybe—but it could be sooner," the lawman said. "Best you get to work on them right now. Want them fed, watered and rubbed down. Mean that for the packhorse, too."

"But, *señor*—I am alone! I am not sure if I—"

He stopped short as Rye dug into a pocket, produced a silver dollar and flipped it to him. The man's attitude changed instantly. He grinned as he caught the coin and bobbed.

"It will be as you say, *señor*. They will all be ready soon."

"Where'll they be?" Rye asked. He was thinking of the possibility of being compelled to leave suddenly in the early hours.

"In these front stalls; I will keep the front one for the bay when the blacksmith is done with him."

The marshal nodded and continued on to the smithy's shop—a shed with an extending roof under which his forge, tools, anvil and several small kegs of shoes were arranged. A squat, thick-shouldered, red-faced man named Decker was the proprietor according to a sign hanging from the canopy.

"Any chance of having him ready by dark?" Rye wanted to know when the blacksmith, pipe in his mouth, examined the bay's hooves.

"No, sir, not a chance," Decker said flatly. "I don't do that kind of no-account work."

"I appreciate that," Rye said. "How long will it take?"

Decker considered the sun. "Well, I expect I can have the job done by eight, maybe nine o'clock. That be soon enough?"

"It will have to be," Rye said. "When he's ready, take him next door to the livery stable. Got my other horses there . . . What's the charge?"

Decker named his price, a bit higher than average, Rye thought, but he made no comment and paid the price. As he turned to go, the pounding of hooves, the rattling of chains and a swirl of dust at the lower end of the street where a crossroads from the east intersected drew his attention. He recalled then seeing the stage depot. Frowning as an idea shaped up in his mind, he glanced at Decker.

"What's the next stop for the stage after it leaves here?"

The blacksmith, in the act of tying Metzgar's horse to a short post, paused. "Santa Fe."

"When does it pull out?"

"Daylight or thereabouts. Stays here overnight. Why? You figuring to leave your horses here and take it?"

"Was just wanting to know," Rye said and moved on. He paused at the livery stable. The hostler was busy with the chestnut and, taking time to pay him in advance for the care of the three horses, continued on to the restaurant. Ordering up an evening meal for Metzgar and himself, the lawman once more returned to the street and made his way to the hotel.

Metzgar was sitting in a rocking chair nursing the bottle of whiskey. He glanced up when Rye entered.

"Everything all right?" he asked, and when Rye nodded the jurist added: "What about the Dixons and the others? Any sign of them?"

"Haven't looked. Was busy getting the horses cared for," the marshal said and, obtaining the telescope from his saddlebags, moved to the lone window of the room and trained the glass on the road to the south.

"See anybody?" Metzgar wanted to know.

"Dust. Could be them or could be somebody else. If it's Dixon and any of the others, they've done some hard riding."

The idea that had stirred through him when he first saw the incoming stagecoach filled John Rye's mind again.

"Think I've got a way to get them off our heels if it is them," he said.

Metzgar's thin face brightened. He set the bottle on a close-by table and brushed at his goatee, now somewhat ragged from lack of care.

"How?"

Rye restored the glass to its place in his saddlebags. "Supper'll be here in a couple of minutes. We'll talk about it then. Means you'll be taking the stage to Santa Fe."

"I'll be going on alone?"

"Just to Santa Fe."

Metzgar swore and reached for the bottle. "Can't

say that I like the idea much. Where'll you be? I sure—"

A knock on the door interrupted the judge. Rye turned at once and crossed to the scarred panel.

"That'll be our suppers," he said.

16

Rye and Asa Metzgar were in the saddle and heading north a full hour before daylight that next morning with the judge constantly mumbling curses at being turned out so early.

"Only thing we could do," Rye said impatiently after listening to the objections for a time. "What you best know is if it wasn't for your sake I sure as hell wouldn't be climbing into a cold saddle at this time of the night!"

"Don't think it was necessary," Metzgar insisted. "We don't know if it was the Dixon bunch or Bedford who rode in."

"Just it: we don't know for certain who it was, but it could have been them—and I'm not taking any chances."

Metzgar glanced back over his shoulder. It was still well before first light and a soft silver glow lay over the land.

"You remember what I told you last night?" Rye asked as the horses, frisky after their rest and feeding, moved on at a good pace. Metzgar had been pretty well liquored up, and the lawman wasn't too sure the judge had gotten things straight.

Metzgar, attention again on the trail ahead, shrugged. "Guess I do. You're putting me on the stagecoach when it comes along, then rigging up some kind of a dummy on my horse."

The lawman nodded. "May be all for nothing, but again I don't like to gamble. We'll stop the stage when it catches up to us. You'll get aboard and ride it to Santa Fe, where you'll have the driver drop you off—"

"At somebody's horse ranch at the edge of town."

"That somebody's name is Jim Russell. Friend of mine. Wife's name is Vergie. Tell Jim I'd like for them to put you up till I come for you—and you're to stay right there, out of sight till I do; that clear?"

Metzgar's shoulders stirred. "Reckon it is."

"The road forks just before we get to Santa Fe. I'll take the left fork for Taos; I aim to make it real easy for anybody following us to see that. You'll be waiting at Jim Russell's on the right fork. It'll take us on to a town called Las Vegas—Vegas to some—where we can get on the Cimarron Cutoff."

"I'm beginning to see it now," Metzgar said. "You and the horses will be on the way to Taos with some kind of a dummy you plan to rig up in my saddle—"

"Using your hat and coat."

"Idea is to make Dixon and Bedford, and those other two, if they're following, think it's Taos we're going to."

Rye grunted in satisfaction. Metzgar, despite the stupor he'd been in, had understood the scheme.

"I'll pull off the road somewhere after I'm certain they're trailing me and let them pass. Then I'll cut back across the hills and meet you at Russell's. If the Dixons and anyone else are following, that should get rid of them; if they're not, all we've lost is a little time—and we can quit worrying about them."

Metzgar had filled his pipe and was puffing slowly at it. "Be a relief to know that. Plan should really work."

"No good reason why it won't. And when we get to

the cutoff we'll keep going till we get to Middle Springs, a place in the southwest corner of Kansas. From there it'll be a straight shot north to Nebraska." Metzgar smiled, nodded. "And all that time that bunch hunting me will be poking around Taos, and maybe Colorado, wondering where I am."

Rye shook his head. He could see a high place in the road in the near distance that would slow the stagecoach. It would be a good place to wait.

"You're forgetting one thing," he warned. "You did a lot of big talking back there in that saloon, told everybody where we were headed. Odds are the Dixons, and for damn sure Jake Bedford, know that. And if that fellow Smith and his partner Pedgett come that way they'll know, too."

"Maybe," the judge said lamely. "Just could be none of them will ask about us."

"That whiskey's pickled your brain if you believe that . . . We'll pull up in that patch of trees on ahead and wait for the stage there."

A half hour later they halted on the shoulder of the road. Rye dismounted at once and turned to Metzgar.

"Take what you figure you'll need till I come for you. Could be two, maybe three days. Have you got another hat and coat?"

"Coat, no hat—"

"I'll need the ones you're wearing. If somebody got a good look at you, they just might be smart enough to notice any change."

Metzgar made no reply but took a second coat from his saddlebag, emptied the pockets of the one he was wearing into it and then handed it along with his low-crowned hat to the lawman. Hanging them on the saddle of the judge's bay, Rye moved off into the trees in search of suitable limbs with which to create the effigy that would represent the jurist.

He located several sticks of the proper length and with bits of rawhide lashed them together, more or less in the shape of a cross with the upright member in the form of a Y. Using more rawhide string, he tied the affair securely to Metzgar's saddle, draped the coat with the crosspiece thrust into the arms. That done, he buttoned the garment to keep it in place and set the judge's hat on the bit of limb extending above the coat's collar. Making certain that all was firmly together, the marshal stepped back and considered his work.

"That maybe'll fool them if they don't get too close," Metzgar said.

"Something I don't aim to let them do," Rye said and turned his attention to the trail. "That stagecoach ought to be showing up."

It had grown steadily lighter as dawn drew near and the land, a broad mesa with scattered juniper trees, bayonet yuccas and a covering of grama grass, was still gentle-looking and quiet. In the distance, and rising up to meet the brightening sky, was the towering mass that was the Sangre de Cristo Mountains, at the base of which lay Santa Fe.

They would be making their way along the east side of the range if all went according to plan, just as the Dixons and the others would be to the west of the range, and no longer of any consequence—at least until they were well into Kansas. Rye was not certain how much distance would lie between them when he and Metzgar reached Kansas, and their pursuers, finding themselves on the wrong trail, began to turn east for the same area, but they would be at least a day, perhaps two, catching up.

"Expect that's the stage coming now," the lawman heard Metzgar say. "Can hear horses. You still think this is a smart idea?"

"I do," Rye said, walking out into the center of the road.

He could see the coach far down the grade and it would be a good quarter hour or so before it reached the crest, but he was taking no chances on the stage's not stopping; he wanted Asa Metzgar aboard and on his way to the New Mexico capital without fail.

The four-hitch came up the slope at a slow trot and drew to a halt when the driver, an elderly, gray-haired man, drew the rig to a stop.

"This here a holdup?" he demanded at a shout, peering down at Rye and the judge. "If'n so you're going to a mess of trouble for nothing. Ain't carrying no strongbox or no mail, either."

"No holdup," Rye assured the man. "Got a passenger for you."

The driver swore in relief. "That's better. Just climb aboard, ain't nobody inside but a whiskey drummer. Where you wanting to go?"

"Not me, it's my friend here," the marshal replied. "You know the Russell place—right outside of town?"

"Jim? Sure do. The company's done some horse-buying business with him."

"My friend wants to be dropped off there."

"Sure enough—but it'll cost him the same as going all the way into town, though."

At that moment the lone passenger, who had evidently been dozing, opened the door of the coach. A heavyset man in a checked suit, he glanced about.

"What's wrong? There some kind of trouble?" he asked in a nasal voice.

"Ain't nothing wrong," the driver answered. "Get back inside, and you, mister, if you're coming, climb aboard. I'll collect what you owe when we get to Russell's."

Metzgar nodded and, saying nothing to John Rye, entered the coach. Before he could close the door the driver had cracked his whip and had the team moving.

Rye remained in the roadway for several moments watching the vehicle disappear in a swirl of dust as it gathered speed on the downgrade of the rise. Turning then to the horses, he tied a lead rope to the judge's bay and, attaching it to a ring on the skirt of his saddle, mounted up and rode on, the packhorse and Metzgar's bay now following contentedly side by side.

The marshal continued through the day, arriving at the fork in the road near dark. Taking the left-hand route which led to Taos, he pressed on for another hour or so and then, halting, made camp near a clump of junipers well back from the road. He saw to the horses first, after which he prepared a quick meal. That over, he walked back to the road and, finding a suitable perch on a rock, listened and studied his back trail for a good half hour. Hearing or seeing nothing that alarmed him, Rye then returned to camp and, rolling up in his blanket, went to sleep.

At first light he was up, made himself a pot of strong coffee, supplemented it with dry bread and jerky and was soon back on the road to Taos. This would be the important day; he would know if the Dixons and Jake Bedford, and the two other men, Smith and Pedgett, were trailing Metzgar and him, and if so, allow them time to see him if his plan to evade them was to work.

They could not be too far behind now, he reasoned, assuming they had been the ones stirring up dust south of Greasewood, and if all went well, he should soon spot them. Readying the horses, he rode to a high place on the trail from which he had a clear view of the fork and where, in turn, anyone arriving at the split in the road would be able to see him, and there built a fire, as if camped.

He hadn't long to wait. Close on to noon three riders broke into view. They didn't pause at the division in the trail but came straight on—an indication they had seen the lawman even before the fork had been reached. There was no sign of any of the others, but most likely Bedford was not far behind. Killing the fire, Rye mounted and rode on.

Satisfaction was running through him. Now he knew where Gar Dixon and his party were. He had been right to take the precautions he had, and there was no longer any need to speculate, to wonder if he and Metzgar were being followed. It surprised him some to find the Dixons ahead of Bedford; he had expected the rancher to be the first on their trail but Gar, his son Devon and Saul Hillman had apparently pushed on without stopping for any length of time. And where were John Smith and Shorty Pedgett?

Part of the question was solved when, late in the afternoon, he swung off into the brushy hills west of the road and, hiding the horses in the dense growth, made his way back to where he had a good view of the trail.

It was near dark when the Dixons passed by—all glum, silent men riding at a fair pace. Their horses looked worn, proof they had been pushed hard that day. Rye watched them disappear, a hard smile on his lips. The plan had worked so far. All he needed now was for Bedford, Smith and Pedgett to put in their appearance.

The former did just that about an hour later. He was astride a big gray gelding that also showed signs of wear. The rancher passed by, as did the Dixons without slowing his pace.

That left only Smith and Pedgett, who might or might not be out to take vengeance on Asa Metzgar; Rye had never fully decided the question. Thinking of it, the lawman changed camps, moving a few miles back down the trail toward Santa Fe to a more suitable location, and there settled down for the night.

When first light came and Smith and his partner had not passed that way, Rye concluded the pair had already passed by or else had taken the Vegas road. Whatever the answer he could not delay any longer and, dismantling the effigy on Metzgar's horse, he started out across country for Santa Fe. He stopped at Jim Russell's ranch for an hour or so, then rejoined the judge and hurried on.

17

Three days later, when they rode into the town of Las Vegas, Metzgar had to admit that John Rye had outsmarted the Dixons as well as Jake Bedford—along with John Smith and Shorty Pedgett, whoever the hell they were. He and the lawman had maintained a close watch on the trail since leaving Santa Fe, and there had been no sign of any of them, an indication that the Dixons and Bedford, at least, had not turned back. As to Smith and Pedgett, they could be anywhere, the lawman felt, but most likely somewhere ahead.

And Rye, cautious as always, chose not to ride directly up to the town's main hotel but to circle the settlement and put up for the night at a small inn at its north end. Perhaps it was because there was a livery stable close by as well as a general store, but regardless, Asa Metzgar did not feel such circumspection was necessary. They had rid themselves of the men who would like to kill him, and as he had never served as a judge in the settlement—although wild and wide open as it was it could use a firm hand on the bench—he was unknown in the area. Thus he could see no good reason why they shouldn't enjoy what the town had to offer. It had been a long, tedious journey from Clear Springs.

"Think I'll just take a walk back to that saloon—the one on the other side of the hotel," he said when they had halted in the runway of the stable. "I know you

like to look the horses over good so there's no use of
me standing around getting in the way."

"No, reckon not," Rye answered in his usual flat
way, knowing full well what was in the judge's mind.
"Sign us in at the hotel when you pass by. Upstairs
room, facing the street."

Metzgar, hanging his and Rye's saddlebags over a
shoulder, laughed. "Front room? Why you being particular? Those Dixons and Jake Bedford are somewhere around Taos now, or maybe halfway into Colorado. No use sweating over—"

"There's still that fellow Smith and Shorty Pedgett,
and are you willing to bet there's nobody around here
aching to gun you down?"

Metzgar shrugged. "Never been in Vegas before,
not even in this part of the territory in fact. Nobody
around here knows me."

Rye sighed. "Like to think that's so, but men travel
around; don't forget that. When you go into that saloon, watch your mouth as well as your step. This is a
tough town."

"Sure, Marshal, and much obliged. Expect I can
take care of myself," Metzgar said stiffly and retraced
his steps back into the bright sunlight.

Making his way to the hotel, the jurist registered the
lawman and himself, obtained the desired front room
and, after tossing the saddlebags on the bed, hastened
back to the street and to the nearby saloon—the Cac-
tus Flower by name.

His supply of whiskey had run dry the previous evening and, bellying up to the bar, where a dozen or so
men were slaking their thirst, he ordered a bottle.
When the bartender, a swarthy black-mustached for-
eigner of some kind with small black eyes, complied,

Metzgar immediately asked for a glass and poured himself a drink. Gulping it down, he smiled at the man behind the counter.

"Long ride from Santa Fe—'specially if a man runs out of liquor—"

The bartender nodded solemnly, took Metzgar's money and returned the change. Elsewhere in the noise-filled saloon a fight had broken out between two men. A woman screamed and there was much yelling back and forth, but the confusion had but small effect on the dark-faced barkeep, who only glanced disinterestedly in the direction of the altercation and then proceeded to serve a customer farther down the bar.

"No law in this town?" Metzgar asked later of the man standing to his right, who had turned and was facing him.

"Sure, only him and his deputy can't be everywhere at once. Too many saloons."

Metzgar wagged his head. "I'd like to be a judge here for about a week. I'd put a stop to this hell-raising."

"You a judge?" the man asked. Tall, with narrow features, dressed in a corduroy suit and a high-crowned, wide-brimmed hat, he nodded slightly when Metzgar offered to refill his empty glass.

"My profession. Name's Asa Metzgar."

Immediately a frown crossed Metzgar's face. The words had come out before he had thought—the very words John Rye had warned him against. But what the hell—there could be very little danger here for him in a strange town, and Jake Bedford and the Dixons were miles away, on the yonder side of the mountains, in fact.

The man voiced his thanks for the liquor, and extended his hand. "I'm Ben Silver. Got myself a ranch east of here. Don't recollect ever hearing your name."

"Not my part of the country. Served in Arkansas, Texas, Arizona and a few other states and territories. Retired now, and I'm on my way home—in Nebraska."

Silver nodded. "Didn't think I'd ever heard the name Metzgar before. Not a common—"

"Well, I have!" a man in range clothing standing just beyond Silver cut in. "Asa Metzgar's a hanging judge —just like that one over in Arkansas."

Silver studied the jurist narrowly. "That right?"

Metzgar downed another shot glass brimming with whiskey. The fight elsewhere in the saloon had ended, and in the sudden quiet that filled the saloon, attention was swinging to the men standing at the bar.

"It has been my job to mete out justice to any criminal brought before me," the judge said in a firm, uncompromising voice. "I'm proud of my record—and proud, too, that I did my best to fulfill my obligation to uphold the law."

"Hell—you strung up just about every man that had the bad luck to face you!"

Metzgar, anger stirring through him, refilled his glass and moved a step back from the counter to where he could see the speaker better.

"I don't think I know you, sir—"

"I ain't never had to stand up in front of you in court, if that's what you mean! But I sure as hell know who you are—and what you are!"

"I did only what my oath and the law expected of me," Metzgar said stiffly.

"The law didn't call for you to hang every man that you judged—and that's just about what you done."

"Now, Austin," Silver said in a placating tone, "you ain't sure of that."

"Like hell I ain't! Couple of friends of mine told me about Metzgar and how he run his court. Folks don't call him a hanging judge for nothing. He's nothing short of a murderer!"

"No—you can't call me that!" Metzgar shouted, face paling. He reached into his coat pocket and grasped the pistol he was carrying. Without drawing it he fired two bullets into Austin.

Echoes shocked the room. Smoke boiled up around the jurist. Austin staggered back, clutching at his side.

"Somebody get the sheriff!" the bartender shouted.

"He ain't in town—"

"Then get the deputy, dammit!"

"Who you best get is Doc Culver," Ben Silver said, supporting Austin's sagging body with an arm. "Don't think he's hurt too bad but he needs attention."

"So does that two-bit hanging judge!" an angry voice in the crowd declared.

"That's right!" someone else cried. "Let's give him a dose of his own medicine!"

Metzgar, pinching out the smoldering fire the bullets he had triggered through his coat pocket, began to back toward the door.

"He didn't even give Austin a chance to go for his gun!"

A chorus of yells filled the saloon at that. Someone said: "Get a rope; we'll show this here hanging judge what it's like to get strung up!"

Asa Metzgar felt his legs tremble. A chill swept through him. The crowd in the saloon meant business.

Sliding his hand into the coat's pocket, he again grasped the pistol. By God, he'd use it again if it became necessary! *Every man had the right to protect himself.* The phrase he'd heard countless times from men who had stood before him, accused of murder, flashed through his mind—usually to no avail. But this was different. This was—

"Where's that rope? Can string him up from that roof beam—"

"What he's got coming, considering all the lynching he's done!"

The sudden blast of a gun sent fresh echoes bouncing about in the saloon again. Metzgar flinched, jerked to one side and turned. Relief surged through him. It was John Rye. Framed in the doorway, hat pushed forward, features rock-hard and grimly set, fringe of his deerskin coat stirring, knuckles of the hand tightly gripping his .45 paper-white, he brought to Asa's mind a painting about an avenging angel he had once seen.

"There'll be none of that!" the lawman shouted into the stillness his gunshot had evoked and fired another bullet into the ceiling to emphasize his words. "I'm a United States marshal. This man is in my custody."

"He up and shot Charley Austin—"

"I'll handle that with your sheriff," Rye said coldly. "Now, all of you back off and go on about your business."

A grumbling came from the crowd but it began to break up. On the opposite side of the room, the piano player had the presence of mind to strike up a tune.

"What's all the shooting?" a man wearing a deputy sheriff's star demanded, coming in from the street.

With him was a much older individual. He was carrying a physician's satchel.

"This here jasper," the man standing beside Austin began, pointing at Metzgar, "up and—"

"Was just an argument, Jess," Ben Silver cut in. "Just sort of got out of hand."

"Hot enough for a shooting," the deputy said dryly, and turned to the judge. Young, dressed in black cord pants, a shield shirt of like color and a high-crowned hat, also black, he was an intense, serious-looking person. "Take that gun out of your pocket—and hand it to me."

"No need for that, Deputy," Rye said quietly. "The man's in my custody. We can talk about it in your office."

Jess turned his attention to the lawman, frowned. "Who're you?"

"U.S. Marshal John Rye."

The deputy's expression changed. He nodded. "I've heard of you . . . All right, long as nobody got killed and you'll be responsible for this man—whoever he is."

"Name's Metzgar, Judge Asa Metzgar," the jurist volunteered. "Expect you've heard of me, too."

Rye swore. "You've got a knack for speaking up and saying the wrong things at the wrong time," he said in a low voice. "Let's get out of here."

Metzgar felt the marshal take him by the arm and, moving past the deputy, conduct him out into the street. Ignoring the dozen or so men loitering about in front of the saloon, he jerked away angrily. Sometimes Rye treated him as if he were a child.

"No need for this. I can walk," he snapped.

Rye made no reply, and in silence they walked

along the street until they reached the hotel. Entering, they went to their room, where the marshal, still silent, settled down into one of the chairs and began to reload his gun. Metzgar, anger waning, crossed to the window and looked out onto the street.

Las Vegas was booming, he'd learned from a conversation overheard while he was standing at the bar in the saloon. Folks were pouring into the town mainly because the railroad was coming. The rumors that had been floating around for years had finally been verified: the Santa Fe was coming. Las Vegas would be a major stop. Already Eastern investors were rushing in to buy land. It was the chance of a lifetime for a man looking for a sure thing.

Metzgar had silently agreed. No doubt Las Vegas offered a fine opportunity for investment, but it was not for him. What future he had lay in Nebraska—in Plattesville. There he could make a new start, get completely away from the law, and lawmen—and criminals. He had enough money salted away in a Denver bank to—

A knock on the door brought Metzgar around just as it got Rye to his feet. The marshal, hand resting on the butt of his revolver as if he expected trouble from the incident in the saloon, crossed to the panel.

"Who is it?" Rye asked.

"It's me, Marshal—Jess—the deputy. Got a lady here who'd like to talk to you."

Metzgar watched Rye wheel to him. Features taut, the lawman's voice was low, barely controlled. "You get yourself mixed up with some woman, too?"

"Hell, no," Metzgar responded angrily. "Never even talked to one."

Rye turned back to the scarred panel and, turning

the key, opened the door. The deputy and a middle-aged woman faced him.

"This here's Mrs. Tuttle, Marshal," the young lawman said. "She's a schoolteacher. Wants to ask you if she can ride along with you to Nebraska."

18

Frustration and impatience gripping him, John Rye
opened the door wider and stepped back to admit the
deputy and the woman. Metzgar had been shooting
off his mouth again; how else did the deputy know
they were headed for Nebraska? Mouth set, he
glanced at the woman. In her late thirties or forties, he
guessed, she had gray-streaked dark hair, faded brown
eyes and a stern mouth. Wearing a high-necked white
shirtwaist and a lead-gray skirt, she looked to be just
what the deputy had said she was: a schoolteacher.

"Why, I don't see why not!" Metzgar said before
Rye could voice a refusal. "The lady's company would
be most welcome."

"Best we give this some thought," Rye said, anger in
his voice. "It's a hard trip, and I don't think we should
expose the lady to the dangers we'll likely run into."

"Dangers? I figure we've put all that behind us,
Marshal . . . Whereabouts in Nebraska are you planning to go, Mrs. Tuttle?"

"A small town near Scottsbluff; I doubt if you've
ever heard of it," the woman replied. She had a pleasant voice and when she spoke, some of the sternness in
her features vanished. "I will be ever so grateful if you
will permit me to accompany you. My mother is seri-
ously ill and I must get to her."

"Best you take the stagecoach," Rye said bluntly,
wishing, as he had before, that Metzgar would keep

his mouth shut. "We'll be going horseback, and traveling hard."

"That will pose no problem, Marshal Rye, I think someone said your name was. I grew up on a ranch and still ride often—and very well. And you are Judge Metzgar," she added, turning to the jurist and extending her hand.

"My pleasure, dear lady," Metzgar said, taking her hand in his and bowing slightly.

"I'm Moriah Tuttle."

"It will be enjoyable having you with us," the judge said. "I'll be looking forward to it."

"You didn't answer my suggestion about the stage," Rye said, irritation sharpening his words. "Why not take it?"

"She can't make the right connections—leastwise without taking a lot of extra time," Jess explained. "If she goes with you she figures she can save three, maybe four, days." The deputy paused, frowned. "Now, if there's any doubt about Mrs. Tuttle, I'll personally vouch for her. So will plenty others around town."

Rye shook his head. "Not doubting the lady. It's just that I don't think it's a good idea. We've had trouble along the way and I'm expecting more before we get to where we're going."

"You have the wrong impression of me, Marshal," the woman said. "At such times I can be an asset. I can shoot just as well as I can ride. My husband taught me how to handle both."

"I'm sure you'd be able to hold up your end," Metzgar said, smiling. "And we can use an extra gun, can't we, Marshal? I vote we let the lady come with us."

"We—me and the whole town—sure will appreciate

it, Marshal," the deputy said. "We all think a lot of Mrs. Tuttle around here, and she needs to get to that town soon as she can."

Moriah Tuttle looked directly into Rye's narrowed eyes. "I won't be any bother to you; I promise that. I'm not the kind of woman who faints at the sight of snakes and spiders—and I'm a good cook. I can take over that chore and relieve you both of it."

Rye glanced toward the window. He didn't like the idea of adding a woman to the party; he was having enough trouble looking after Asa Metzgar without complicating the task with a female.

"What do you say, Marshal?" the deputy pressed. "Mrs. Tuttle has to get there and she can't make the trip on horseback alone. Too many things can happen to a woman by herself."

Rye gave in reluctantly. He was thoroughly against the idea, but Moriah Tuttle evidently did need help in getting to her sick mother, in bad shape, perhaps even dying. Too, they'd only be on the trail for two weeks, more or less, and it appeared they might have shaken the Dixons and the others and would have no further problems with them; at least he hoped so.

"All right," he said, bringing his attention back to the woman. "We'll be moving out at first light. Be at the livery stable, ready to travel."

Moriah Tuttle was on time. When John Rye and Asa Metzgar came out of the hotel and made their way to the barn where they had left their horses, she was already there, astride a husky little black mare with full saddlebags and blanket roll securely in place behind the cantle. She was wearing a pair of men's corduroy pants cut down to proper size, a heavy linsey-woolsey shirt, boots, wool jacket and a narrow-brimmed hat that was pulled well down on her head.

"Good morning," Metzgar greeted. "Looks like you're ready to travel."

"I am," the woman replied, her eyes on the marshal. There was a measure of anxiety in her manner as if she feared the lawman might yet change his mind and refuse her permission to accompany him and the judge.

"Good," Metzgar said cheerfully. "We'll be ready to move out as soon as we get our horses."

Rye, entering the stable, returned shortly leading his chestnut and the packhorse. Metzgar, seeing that the lawman was not also bringing his bay, hurried into the shadow-filled building to get the animal himself.

Rye, going up into the saddle, settled himself and considered Moriah Tuttle, her horse and gear critically. "You got a slicker?"

The woman nodded. "Inside my blanket roll."

The marshal shook his head. "After this wrap it around the roll or carry it in your saddlebags where it'll be handy," he said brusquely. "Rains come up sudden in this country . . . You sure you want to do this? Last chance to call it off."

Moriah shrugged. "I have to do it, Marshal. Please don't worry about me; I can take care of myself."

"You'll have to do just that, Mrs. Tuttle," the lawman said bluntly. "I've got my hands full with Metzgar," he added, watching the judge emerge from the stable with his horse.

"You don't like me much, do you, Marshal?" the woman continued.

"Haven't known you long enough to answer that—and it's not a matter of whether I like you or not. What it boils down to is that I've got a job to do, and your being along is going to make it harder."

"I'll keep out of your way—and I won't be any bother," Moriah said, repeating herself. "And I can be useful, you'll see."

"Can only hope so," Rye said and, as Metzgar climbed up into his saddle, they swung off into the street and onto the trail north.

They rode in silence through the cool predawn for the first hour. The land to their right was green and fresh while the meadowlike area off to the opposite side, from which the town took its name, was a sea of gently stirring grass. On beyond the vast swale, the mighty Sangre de Cristo reached upward with their snowy peaks as if struggling to pierce the brightening blue sky. Well on ahead, the Turkey Mountains formed a gray backdrop to Fort Union, known by one and all as the queen of the forts.

They camped that night along the Mora River, near enough to the fort to hear the sound of bugles and an occasional shout as soldiers went about their duties. Moriah insisted on taking over as camp cook, a job which Rye relinquished without protest. The meal was an excellent one—fried meats, potatoes, corn, greens, biscuits and coffee—and when it was over the two men, following their usual habit of washing their own plates and other utensils, were halted by Moriah as they prepared to do so.

"That's my job," she said. "You go on about whatever else needs doing."

Metzgar grinned as he faced Rye. "Told you she'd be a big help, didn't I? We can forget about cooking and washing dishes. Always said it paid to have a woman around."

The lawman nodded, turned to the woman, who at the moment was scraping scraps into the nearby brush for the small varmints and birds to find.

"Was a fine supper, Mrs. Tuttle," he said. "Want to thank you."

A startled look crossed Moriah's lined features as if she were greatly surprised at the compliment. She smiled.

"Thank you, Marshal. I'll do better after we sort of get strung out and organized."

"You can't do much better than that," Metzgar said, emptying his cup of coffee and pouring a generous measure of whiskey from his bottle into it. "Was as good a meal as a man can buy in any restaurant."

Moriah said, "Thank you, Judge," in a low voice and turned away to complete her chores.

Rye had moved off, walking to where the horses were picketed. Taking the telescope from his saddlebags, and with Metzgar at his side, he crossed to where he had a long view of the country they had just traversed.

"You see anybody coming?" the jurist asked after Rye had spent several moments studying the land.

The lawman shook his head. "A wagon, a patrol of soldiers headed for the fort—that's all."

"Wasn't expecting you to see the Dixons or Jake Bedford. That scheme of yours sure worked fine. They're clear over on the other side of the mountains."

"They'll be there for a while, anyway," Rye said. He was wondering about John Smith and Shorty Pedgett; where were they? Could they be on the trail ahead somewhere?

"Sure glad we let that woman come along," he

heard Metzgar say. "Kept my eye on her all day. She's a good rider. And nothing seemed to bother her. And as for cooking she's—"

"Sounds like you're taking a big interest in her," the marshal said and closed the telescope.

"I just might at that," Metzgar said, sipping at his cup of whiskey. "From what I've seen of her so far, a man sure couldn't do much better."

"Maybe you're right, but being around her for one day is hardly a basis on which to form an opinion."

Metzgar swore angrily. "I might've expected you to say something like that! Been told you never let anybody get close to you, and you never give much of yourself, either. Must be a hell of a poor way to live. Me, I either like somebody or I don't, first off—quick judgment—that's the way I am."

Which could be partly the cause for all the enemies the judge had, Rye thought, but he said nothing and, shrugging, returned to the camp.

Next morning, after a good breakfast designed to carry them through the day till supper, they were again on the trail. Rye, uneasy for some reason, continually scanned the country behind them with his telescope. There were other pilgrims on the road, headed north or south, but none were of interest to him.

Around noon, as they rested their horses in the shade of some trees growing along the fringe of a hilly area, two riders moving north did arouse his interest. He swore softly. Hunched nearby, back against one of the trees, Metzgar looked up quickly.

"What is it?"

"Two riders. I think it's Smith and Pedgett."

Metzgar got to his feet and crossed to where Rye

was studying the distant pair. "Thought we'd lost them a long time ago."

Rye nodded. "Was my thinking too. Looks like the talking you did back there in that saloon's got us in a fix again," he said and turned back to Moriah Tuttle and the horses.

"We're pulling out. Aim to leave the main road here and angle west. There's a town called Goldenrod not too far."

"Why? Is there something wrong?" Moriah, sitting on a stump just within the small grove, asked as she hurriedly got to her feet.

"Can't be sure. But there are a couple of men coming this way that might mean trouble."

"You could do like I said before: use your gun on them," Metzgar said as he mounted.

The marshal ignored the question and swung up into his saddle. The woman, climbing onto her horse, also turned and stared off in the direction of the road. "Are they after you?"

"Maybe, but most likely it's the judge they want. Either way I'd as soon not meet up with them," Rye said and, swinging the chestnut about, cut deeper into the brush and struck a course northwest.

He continued on for a short distance and, when a faint smudge of smoke appeared in the distance, drew to a halt.

"That'll be Goldenrod. No need to go there; just needed to get my bearings. We can wait here until we see what Smith and Pedgett do. If they keep going up the trail, fine."

"Then what?" Metzgar wanted to know.

"We'll camp here for the night, let them get a half

day ahead of us and move on in the morning. If they turn off, follow our tracks—"

"We'll have to shoot it out with them, right?"

"No, we'll go on into Goldenrod, let the law take care of them," Rye said.

"What the hell, Marshal," Metzgar said in disgust, "you're the law."

"Know that—and being the law is what keeps me from killing them. Far as I'm concerned they're not outlaws."

Metzgar scrubbed at his beard. "I think you hold the law too high, Marshal. "You're too careful about upholding it."

"Maybe so, Judge, but I've got to know I'm right before I use my gun on a man . . . Might as well climb down. We'll be here for a spell."

19

"There they are," Asa Metzgar said, moving up to Rye.

The marshal, leaning against a pine tree, turned his eyes to the road. The day was growing old and while it was still several hours until darkness, a late-afternoon haze hung over the land. Raising his glass, Rye focused it on the oncoming riders. They were near enough now to accurately determine their identities.

"Pedgett and Smith, all right," he murmured, confirming his earlier belief.

"Let me have a look," Metzgar said.

Earlier he had been sitting on a log with Moriah Tuttle, regaling her with details of the altercation with Austin that he'd had in the saloon. "Man called me a vile name. Had no choice but to shoot him," Rye heard the judge say in a proud sort of voice.

Relinquishing the glass to the jurist, the lawman waited while Metzgar studied the riders. "Know them?" he asked after a minute or so had elapsed.

Metzgar shook his head and returned the telescope. "Sure don't seem to be anybody I know—but that's understandable. There've been so many men come before me in the last twenty years that I can't expect to remember them all."

"Wait until they get closer," the lawman said. "Can get a better look."

"No need. I don't recognize them."

"Do you think we'll have to ride on to that town?" Moriah asked.

"I'm hoping not—"

"If the marshal wasn't so particular about using that gun he carries, we'd not have all that bother," Asa Metzgar said, voice tinged with sarcasm. "It's only after a crime's been committed that he believes in using it."

John Rye didn't bother to comment. He had already expressed himself on the subject to Metzgar and saw no need to repeat himself. As for Moriah Tuttle, she could believe what she wished, he could care less. Crossing to the horses he took up the lines and, with the packhorse following, moved deeper into the trees.

"Where we going?" the judge asked as he and the woman also mounted. "Thought you said—"

"Just want to get farther back from the road and in behind the brush. Don't want them to see us," Rye said patiently.

"We're going to a lot of extra work for nothing," the judge grumbled. "If you'd settle with them right now they'd be out of our hair for good."

"Forget it!" Rye snapped, temper finally rising. "We let them pass, and that's it!"

He rode on for a few more yards and drew in behind a thick stand of oak brush and false sage. "They won't be able to see us from the road here," he said, dismounting.

Metzgar, features angry, stopped beside the woman as she pulled up. Coming off his horse at once, he began to talk to her in a low, bitter voice. Asa had become increasingly friendly with the woman since leaving Las Vegas, and she appeared to reciprocate his attention. That suited John Rye; it kept Metzgar out of the way a good bit of the time, spared him listening to the judge's complaining and opinions.

The two riders drew abreast. Well hidden, Rye used his glass again, not for the purpose of identifying them —he was already sure of that—but to see if they turned off or continued on the main road. At that moment Metzgar came to his side.

"Like to look at them again—"

The marshal surrendered the telescope to the jurist. Metzgar studied the pair briefly, shook his head. "Nope, sure now that I don't know them."

It wouldn't have mattered to John Rye one way or the other. He was taking no chances and he fully intended to allow the pair to pass, get out ahead of him and resume the trail the following morning. He came back to the horses, glancing about as he did.

"Might as well make camp here," he said. "As good a place as we'll find."

It would be a dry camp as there was no spring or creek anywhere nearby, but that was of no concern. They had an ample supply of water and could refill the canteens later when they reached one of the streams that crossed the trail. Seeing Rye with the horses, Metzgar and Moriah joined him and began to set up camp.

"Heard you say those two might be after you," the judge said a time later, when the evening meal was over and they were enjoying a second cup of coffee. "You think that's maybe true? I expect you've got as many enemies as I have."

"No doubt of it," the lawman said dryly. "And if they want me they'll have to track me down. I don't aim to be bothered now. Thing I want to do is get you to Nebraska and off my hands."

Metzgar's hostile mood seemed to change at mention of his homeland. He sighed deeply. "Sure will be glad to get there. Plattesville is going to look mighty good to me after all these years. And I'm sure anxious to see my farm; it's right close to town."

Rye frowned. "Did you mention that to anybody in that Vegas saloon—or maybe earlier?"

Metzgar stroked his shapeless beard. "No, don't think so. What difference would it make? I'll be home, among folks I know—and that know me." He paused, glanced at Moriah. "You'll like it there."

The woman nodded slightly. She had finished with the evening chores and was sitting on her blanket roll, idly toying with a bit of cloth she held in her hands.

"It's fine country," Metzgar continued. "I aim to get back to farming, not in a big way, but enough to keep me busy. Not going to be a judge anymore—not even if they should ask me. I'm just going to sit back, let things grow and take it easy."

Rye shrugged as he lit up one of his stogies. "Hope that's the way it works out for you."

"Why can't it?"

"Any man wanting to settle a score with you just might learn where you are and come calling."

"Not much afraid of that happening. And like I said, I'll be among friends."

"That won't make much difference to men like Gar Dixon or Jake Bedford. They've got enough hate burning inside them to follow you to hell. There's no hiding from their kind."

"Don't you think you've thrown them off the judge's trail?" Moriah asked.

"Sidetracked them, that's about all, but we can't be

sure of that if they know where we're headed. The judge talks too much at times."

Metzgar tossed aside the dregs of coffee in his cup and replaced them with a measure of whiskey. "Hell, Dixon and them are a long way from here—sweating it out over in New Mexico, or maybe even Colorado by now. Probably don't know which way to go next," he said in a confident tone. "And even if they knew we were going to Nebraska they'd have a hard time getting there."

"Is that right, Marshal?" Moriah wanted to know.

Rye blew a cloud of smoke and watched it break up and disappear in the cool air. "They can get there, all right," he said. "Cut across the top of New Mexico and ride east till they come to Kansas. Then it's straight north to Nebraska."

"Which would take a lot of time," Metzgar pointed out.

"I reckon it will—all depending on where in New Mexico they realized they were on the wrong trail. If they figured it out by the time they got to Taos, they're a lot closer than if they'd kept going north. There's a trail through the mountains there that would put them on this side of the range."

Metzgar shook his head. "Got my doubts they did that. My guess is right now they're somewhere in Colorado, or mighty close to it—and wondering which direction we went."

Rye hoped that was the way of it, but if Asa had done his usual amount of talking when he was back in the saloons along the way, he doubted it. The Dixons and Jake Bedford might be off their trail at the time but they would know where Metzgar could ultimately be found.

"Been trying to talk Moriah here into staying with me in Plattesville, once she's settled her affairs," the judge said. "We've gotten to know each other pretty well since leaving Vegas."

Rye glanced at the woman. She was smiling faintly. "I am considering the offer," she admitted. "It would be nice to have a husband again—and a real home."

Evidently Moriah Tuttle's husband was dead; Rye couldn't recall what, if anything, had been mentioned about the matter. "I wish you luck," he said, "and all—"

"Oh, it's not settled yet," Asa cut in, "but I do hope to have Moriah convinced by the time we reach Nebraska."

A light rain greeted them that next morning shortly after they rode out, but it lasted for only an hour or so, and traveling was not uncomfortable. Rye, using his telescope, was able to get a glimpse of Smith and Shorty Pedgett several times during the next three days, which strengthened his belief that they, too, were heading for Nebraska.

It wasn't the most consoling of thoughts, having two men in front of him, and the possibility of four more somewhere behind, all bent on taking Asa Metzgar's life and his perhaps as well, but he pressed on steadily. He was anxious to get the jurist to Plattesville and thus complete the job assigned him.

They reached the edge of Indian Territory commonly called No Man's Land, angled across it and arrived one afternoon at the place known to travelers as Middle Springs, in Kansas. Rye felt better; a straight shot north and they'd be in Nebraska—a week's journey at most if all went well.

Gar Dixon, squatting on his heels, a cup of chicory in his hand, spat disgustedly into the fire. He didn't know how that lawman and the judge had managed it, but they'd thrown him and Devon and Saul off their trail. Hell only knew how much time they'd lost—a'plenty for sure. But they were on the right track now, he was sure of that. Dixon glanced up as his son threw a handful of dry wood onto the fire, creating an explosion of sparks.

"How far ahead of us do you reckon they are, Pa?" Devon asked.

"Hell, I don't know!" Gar snapped impatiently. "A whole day at least—maybe more."

Saul Hillman, nursing his chicory with both hands wrapped about the tin cup, stared moodily into the fire. It was cold in the high country of northeastern New Mexico and a steadily rising wind was making things worse.

"I'm about ready to call it quits," he announced. "We ain't fixed to be traveling country like this. A man could freeze to death up here."

"Can't quit now," Gar said testily. "Couple of days and we'll for sure be in Kansas. According to that map that fellow showed me back in Taos, it won't be far then to Nebraska, and that town the judge and that lawman are heading for—three or four more days at most."

"Adds up to a week, maybe more," Hillman said dejectedly. "Sure wish I hadn't come along on this wild-goose chase. You told me we'd be gone from home ten days at most. Instead it's getting close to a month."

"Dammit, Saul—just you go ahead and quit! Next

town we come to I want you to turn back; I'm tired of your bellyaching."

"Ain't got much cash, you know that. We're even running out of grub—and you ain't got no money either."

"Can sell your horse and tack, raise some cash that way. Then buy yourself a ticket on a stagecoach."

Hillman gave that thought. Off in the clear, cold night a coyote barked into the silver glow of the moon, immediately received an answer from another of his kind farther away.

"No, reckon not," he said, pulling his coat closer about his body. "I told Sadie I'd stick with you till you got all that vengeance out of your craw. Aim to stand by my word."

Gar stiffened and his brow darkened. "Well, now, if you think you're bound to hang around just because my old woman asked you to, just forget it! Me and Devon can do what has to be done."

"But you ain't even sure where Metzgar is—and you're only guessing where he's going. Nebraska is a mighty big place, I hear."

"Ain't big enough for him to hide from me in. I'll root him out even if I have to track him clean to Canada."

"Just might be where you'll end up—if you don't get your head blowed off first. That lawdog watching over Metzgar means business."

Gar turned his head aside and spat. "Don't fret none over that; I can handle him."

"Maybe. I keep remembering what the sheriff in Socorro told us about him, and I'm sort of believing it."

"Lawdog talk!" Gar said derisively and spat again. "They look out for each other that way—always saying

how tough and mean one of their kind is. Ain't nothing
but talk . . . Any more of that java, Devon?"

"No, Pa. Pot's bone-dry."

"Then I reckon we might as well turn in," Gar said,
getting to his feet. "I sure hope it's warmer in Kansas."

20

"Expect there's some things we're running short of, Mrs. Tuttle," Rye said, halting at a trader's wagon pulled up alongside the trail. "Whatever we need, we best get it here. Probably be our last chance until we get to Plattesville," he added as he swung down from the saddle. Nearby Moriah and Asa Metzgar were also dismounting.

"You reckon he's got any liquor?" the judge said in a hopeful voice.

Rye shrugged. "Some do . . . Mrs. Tuttle, when you do your buying, add about forty pounds of grain for the horses. Tell the sutler I'll settle with him when you're done . . . Judge, give her a hand."

Metzgar turned and immediately hurried off after the woman. Rye, taking his telescope, moved off to one side and turned the glass northward along the trail they would be following. There was no one in sight. Coming about, the lawman studied the road to the east.

There were several riders to be seen along with a half dozen or so wagons. The latter were all moving slowly westward on the trail. A few of the men on horseback were heading in a like direction, but the majority of those visible were heading east for Dodge City. Rye studied each paired-off couple intently, searching for John Smith and Shorty Pedgett, but could not locate them.

Frowning, he gave that thought. Were they so far ahead that his glass could not pick them up? He doubted that. The two men would have traveled at about the same pace as he and his party. Turning back to the trail north, he carefully scanned it once again. The result was the same: he could see no riders, but the slightly rolling contour of the land could conceal travelers, he realized. He'd have another look a little later on; meanwhile he'd talk to the sutler.

Returning to the horses, Rye restored the glass to its place in his saddlebags and crossed to the trader's wagon. Moriah had completed her purchasing and the sutler, a lanky, red-faced man in overalls and dark blue shirt, was just placing the items in a box. Off to one side Metzgar, his bottle replenished from the keg the sutler carried, was hunched on his heels waiting for the transaction to be completed. Near him was the sack of grain Rye had ordered.

"You the man that pays off? " the sutler asked smilingly as Rye approached.

The lawman nodded. "Everything but the whiskey," he said, as Moriah and Metzgar gathered up her purchases and headed back to the horses.

"Your friend done paid for it," the sutler said. "He didn't figure you'd want to."

"He was right," Rye answered and, glancing at the bill the sutler handed him, paid over the amount stated for the grub and grain.

"You see two men pass by here going north?" he asked, lighting up a cigar. "Would've probably been early today."

The sutler shook his head. "Sure didn't. Ain't been nobody heading that way since I've been here—four days now."

"Could they have gone by maybe in the dark and you wouldn't have seen them?"

"Sure misdoubt that," the trader said and pointed to a large dog lying under the wagon. "I tie him up to a wheel at night. Raises holy hell if somebody comes up close. Course, they could have circled past me during the dark."

Rye considered the sutler's words. What had happened to Smith and Pedgett? He could not have overtaken them on the trail—and there was no sign of them anywhere—and the trader was certain they had not passed by going north. Maybe the two men were just on the move, drifters, who had no interest in Metzgar, or him. It sounded logical and was most comforting.

"Them two fellows—they friends of yours?"

"No, just a couple I know that I figured passed this way . . . The country north of here—to Nebraska—is new to me. Don't know what to expect. Will we have any trouble finding water?"

The sutler leaned back against the side of his wagon. The day was beginning to cool and a wind had sprung up.

"Dang it," he muttered, "looks like we're in for another blow tonight . . . But you're wanting to know about the country—just about the same as it is around here, flat, gullies and maybe a deep wash now and then. Ain't a lot of trees and brush, but there's some. And there ain't much of a trail, but riding horseback you won't have no trouble."

"What about water?" Rye repeated his question.

"Well, you'll come to the Cimarron River about ten mile on. Twenty miles farther on you'll cross what folks call the North Fork, then it'll be dry till you get to the Arkansas."

"How far?"

"Be fifty mile or so. Best you fill up good there because the next place you can water will be the Smoky Hill River, sixty, maybe seventy mile on. After that you won't have no trouble. There's the Upper Fork of the Smoky less'n a day's ride and then you'll hit Beaver Creek, which oughtn't to be dry right now. After that you'll come to the Republican, which is a pretty fair river. Just follow it right on into Nebraska and you'll reach the Platte—"

"Won't have any trouble once we're there. Man with me knows that part of the country. What about Indians?"

"Ain't been no trouble lately, but a man never knows when he might run into a party of renegade Arapahos. Just have to keep your eyes peeled."

"Goes for about anywhere," Rye said. "Sure obliged to you."

"It's me that's obliged to you for your business," the trader said, extending his hand. "Now, if you're looking for a right good place to camp, just keep going till you come to the Cimarron. Plenty of grass for your horses and you'll find all the firewood you need along the river."

"Obliged to you again," Rye said, shaking the trader's hand and turning toward the horses.

"If them two friends of yours shows up you want me to tell them where you'll be?" the sutler called.

"No," Rye answered without looking back. "Expect they went on to Dodge City. I'll look them up next time I'm there."

It was a comfortable camp that night along the qui-

etly flowing Cimarron, and the next day they continued on across the grassy land, broken only occasionally
by solitary clumps of brush or a tree, growing usually
along a low bluff or in one of the countless shallow
washes. They passed up the North Fork after watering
the horses and refilling their canteens and made a
night stop in a coulee not many miles north of it.

Rye was becoming more anxious to reach Nebraska,
where he could deliver Asa Metzgar to his destination.
He was weary of looking after his charge, of the endless miles in the saddle and of having to be forever
alert for the men seeking vengeance on the judge—
not to mention the possibility of encountering hostile
Indians.

He was grateful now that Moriah Tuttle had become
a member of the party. She and Metzgar had become
closer, which had resulted in the jurist's being much
less trouble than he'd been at the start. Too, it kept the
woman occupied. The pair appeared to enjoy one another's company and spent most of the time riding
side by side, or sitting together at night after the meal
was over and they were all gathered by the fire.

There were several parties camped along the banks
of the Arkansas when they arrived there, and Rye
avoided all. He was never certain when they might
come upon a man with a grudge against Asa Metzgar
—whose enemies seemed countless and on hand at
every turn. Too, he was certain they had not seen the
last of Gar Dixon and his party, or of Jake Bedford.
Sooner or later he was sure they would turn up; it was
just a matter of when.

The river was low at that time of year and, crossing
it at one of the several fords, they halted in a place well
apart from the others and there spent the night.

By daybreak they were on their way again, all now showing signs of travel. Rye and the packhorse were in the lead, as was customary, Metzgar and Moriah Tuttle riding together, slightly behind and to the lawman's left, apparently at a distance where their conversation could not be overheard.

The marshal thought little of it and took no offense. Maybe the Hanging Judge and the schoolteacher could make a life for themselves on his Nebraska farm. He hoped so for the woman's sake, but he had his doubts that Asa Metzgar's past would ever allow him to know peace.

On one day short of reaching the Nebraska border Rye spotted three riders coming up from the south. They were well in the distance and he could discern very little about them. He was more disturbed by a party of four headed east out of Colorado, and a lone rider coming from the direction of Dodge City. All would bear watching as closely as possible, and throughout that day he continually turned his glass on them.

"Something bothering you?" Metzgar asked during one of the times when they halted in the shade of a tree or a bluff to rest the horses.

"Riders. Coming toward us from three sides. Don't know if they're looking for you or not."

"Couldn't they just be pilgrims going somewhere?" Moriah asked, a worried look on her usually bland features.

"Maybe. Need to keep an eye on them just the same. We'll camp ahead a few more miles; that sutler said there'd be a creek along here somewhere."

"How much farther to the Platte River?" Moriah wanted to know.

"The marshal figures we've got about a day yet till we come to the Nebraska border. Then it'll take three more to reach Plattesville—and home. Expect you're mighty tired of that saddle."

"I am," Rye heard the woman say in a worn voice.

They made camp in a small grove of trees along the creek, picketing the horses near the shallow stream a few yards below. As it had been almost from the beginning, there was only a brief period of conversation after the meal was finished and coffee was being had by the fire, before, tired from the long day, they sought out their blankets and tarps.

Rye was always the last to turn in, feeling it necessary to have a good look and listen around the camp for anything that might indicate trouble. Too, the marshal enjoyed the few minutes of solitude under the star-filled sky during which he could gaze out over the endless plains, soft silver-gray in the star- and moonlight, and hear the muted, comforting sounds of the small creatures that rustled about in the night.

Circling the camp again, the lawman then moved off a short distance to a low hill, in reality only a high place on the flat plain, and studied the country to the south and west for a red glow that would indicate a campfire. He could see none, and after a time he cut back to where Metzgar and Moriah Tuttle were sleeping. Their own fire was now but glowing embers, and as he passed silently to where his blanket and tarp lay, a sound in the thick brush on the opposite side of the camp brought him to sharp attention.

Dropping back instantly, he drew his gun and began to work his way quietly through the trees and undergrowth. It hardly seemed possible any of the riders he had seen could have caught up with them, but by traveling hard and keeping out of sight, he reckoned it could be done.

Rye halted abruptly. There was movement ahead—just beyond a clump of brush. The lawman glanced toward the center of camp. He could see Asa Metzgar rolled up in his blanket and tarp near the faintly glowing fire, proof that it could not be the judge up and on his feet for one reason or another. From where he stood he could see only a part of Moriah Tuttle's bed, as she had laid it off to one side.

Thumb on the hammer of his gun, forefinger against the trigger, Rye moved up to the stand of brush. Reaching its edge, he paused and then stepped quickly around it. The shadow he had seen whirled with a startled gasp. It was Moriah Tuttle.

Rye swore angrily and then, as tension drained from his taut frame, he slid his weapon back into its holster. "What the hell are you doing prowling around in the dark like this?" he demanded.

The woman trembled. She was clutching a small-caliber, nickel-plated pistol and, in the pale light threading its way down through the trees, her face was tightly drawn and white as the robe she had pulled on over her clothing.

"I—I thought I heard something—someone—"

Rye swore again. "Best you leave something like that up to me; you could get yourself killed."

"What's the trouble?" Metzgar, evidently aroused by their voices, called.

"Go back to sleep," Rye answered. "We thought we heard something."

"We? You mean Moriah's there with you?" Metzgar shouted, coming to his feet. Throwing a hasty glance to where the woman had her blanket and canvas, he shook his head. "Hell, I never heard a thing."

"Could have been a deer or maybe a coyote," Rye said. "Go on back to bed, I'll have another look around."

"I guess we're all sort of edgy," Metzgar said, "but I guess it's natural, going through all that we have. Just glad we're this close to home, and it'll all be over in a few more days."

Rye made no comment but remained where he was as he thoughtfully watched the woman return to her bed. For an intelligent woman, she had done a very foolish thing, and he wondered if she realized it.

After a few moments he turned away and began to circle the area around the camp once more on the chance there was someone prowling about. Most likely it had been a deer or perhaps a coyote, but it always paid to make sure.

21

"Going to have to hold up a spell," Rye said that next morning not long after they had moved out. "Pack-horse is walking lame."

Halting, he came off the saddle and dropped back to where the bay was standing. Nearby Metzgar and Moriah Tuttle turned to watch.

"It something serious?" the judge asked.

Rye, in the act of examining the bay's left foreleg, shook his head. "Can't say. There's some swelling, but I can't find a cut."

"Probably bruised," Metzgar said. "Once had a horse that kept hitting the back of his front leg with his hind hoof. Forging, I think the horse doctor called it."

"What did he say to do about it?"

"Had me fix a sort of leather boot to protect the leg."

Rye nodded. He had no leather, at least not a piece large enough to go around the bay's fetlock, but he guessed he could use cloth wound tight and secured with rawhide string. But first he should take care of the swelling.

"Wait here," he said to Metzgar and the woman, "I'll take the bay down to the creek. Want to pack his leg with mud before I wrap it."

Metzgar glanced off in the direction of the trail. "Nobody in sight. You figure there's any need to keep on watching the road behind us?"

"It is—until we get to Plattesville," Rye said flatly and, mounting his horse, headed back for the creek with the bay trailing faithfully along at his side.

It required a little more than a half hour to scrape up sufficient mud for a poultice and pack it around the horse's fetlock, where it was held in place by a bit of canvas and some rawhide string; but the loss of time worried John Rye nevertheless, and when the party was once more on the move northward, he continually looked back over the route they had come, occasionally using his telescope, for signs of anyone following. His search was never rewarded but that did not dispel the uneasiness in the lawman that had begun to nag at him in the past few hours.

He could no longer locate the three riders he'd spotted coming up from the south, and that disturbed him most of all. The quartet angling toward them from Colorado were now well off to the side and appeared to be heading for some point in the northeastern corner of that state. The solitary horseman coming from the direction of Dodge City was still to be seen well to the east, but he, too, looked to have a definite direction in mind, perhaps in Dakota, on beyond Nebraska. There was a lot of work there, the marshal had heard, and in hard times such would draw men looking for a job from many areas.

Rye dismissed the quartet and the single rider from his mind just as he had dismissed John Smith and Shorty Pedgett, who certainly would have made their move days ago if they had been planning an ambush. If there was to be trouble, it would most likely come from the three riders his constant surveillance could no longer turn up. They could be the Dixons, and if so Gar was taking pains to keep out of sight.

Of course he could be entirely wrong as to their identity. He was basing his suspicions on the knowledge that the Dixons, three in number, had apparently been trailing them since they left Socorro, far back in New Mexico Territory. He had managed to shake them at Santa Fe, sending them on northward to Taos, but whether they had kept going or discovered they had been tricked and doubled back to get on the Las Vegas road, he had no way of knowing.

Either way, there had been three riders behind them on a seldom-used trail, and now they had disappeared in a part of the country where there were no settlements, and therefore no reason to drop from sight.

The more Rye thought about it the less he liked the feel of it and, as they worked steadily on, the belief in his mind grew to where it was almost a conviction: it was the Dixons. But he said nothing of it to Metzgar or the woman. There was no need to alarm them, if indeed such information would. Riding along side by side, occasionally holding hands and carrying on a continual conversation, they seemed totally oblivious to the world around them.

The country had changed little since Middle Springs—endless gentle rolls and flats of grassland, scattered trees, occasional stands of brush, red buttes, and wide, lumpy-looking areas of prairie dog villages. It was pleasantly cool and the horses, fed a ration of grain and continually afforded good grazing each day, were, except for the packhorse, in excellent condition after so long a journey. But even the little bay was in fine shape, his wounded leg having improved greatly.

At midday they reached the river the sutler had called the Republican. Stopping there, they ate a bit of lunch and while the horses rested, Rye stepped out into the clear where he could scan their back trail. Again he failed to turn up any indication of being followed, but now the possible reason for such had become more apparent.

The land to the west had dropped off and a fairly deep swale had taken over. Men riding in the depression would not be readily visible to anyone on the road except at irregular periods. Taking that into consideration, the lawman spent even more time searching the country behind them, but to no avail. It was as if there were no Dixons or anyone else to beware of.

Anyone else? Jake Bedford—what of him? Was he somewhere back on the plains endeavoring to catch up and settle his fancied wrong with Asa Metzgar, too? Or had he, wounded in the saloon back in Greasewood, used good sense when he discovered he was on the wrong trail out of Santa Fe and given up on his thirst for vengeance? Rye hoped so. The Dixons would be enough to cope with if—and when—they showed up.

They camped that night on the upper Republican River, not far from the Nebraska border. It was a brushy area with many trees, and by far the best place for an overnight stop they had come to since leaving the Cimarron.

Unloading the packhorse for Moriah and building a fire for her use, Rye, still uneasy, took the glass from his saddlebags and, as Metzgar led the animals off for feeding and watering, made his way to a ridge a short distance away. Halted there he turned the telescope to the south, looking for a campfire, for smoke, or anything that might reveal the presence of anyone pursuing them.

Darkness had come early, thanks to a heavy overcast that had moved in late in the day. He saw no evidence of anyone and, closing the telescope, turned, started back to camp. Abruptly he came to a halt. Three shadowy figures, barely visible in the swiftly closing night, were entering the brushy grove some fifty yards or so below. The Dixons! It could be no one else.

Crouched low, Rye left the rise at a run. Reaching the camp, he found Moriah busy at the fire preparing the evening meal. Metzgar had finished his chores with the horses and was laying out his bed.

"Want you both over there in that thick stand of brush—quick!" the lawman said in a taut voice as he pointed to the upper side of the small clearing they were in. "Get there and stay down low!"

The woman came upright, the flickering flames reflecting on her placid features, question in her eyes. Metzgar, abandoning his sleeping preparations, hurriedly crossed over to where the lawman stood.

"What is it?"

"Three men coming this way through the trees," Rye said tersely. "I expect it's the Dixons."

The judge reached into a pocket for his gun. "Hell, I can—"

"Forget it!" Rye snapped. He had little faith in Metzgar's ability to handle a weapon safely and efficiently. "Keep in the brush till I come for you."

Saying no more, the marshal moved off into the semidarkness of the grove in the direction he figured the three men would be coming from. His weapon was out and ready, and the tenseness that had possessed him was now gone, leaving him cool and composed. He'd hoped to avoid any showdown with the

Dixons—if it was them, and who else could it be?—but they were determined to force his hand, it appeared, and he had no choice but to use his gun.

"Can't see nothing, Pa—"

The voice was that of Devon Dixon. At once Gar, speaking in a hoarse whisper, replied.

"Well, they're there all right. We spotted them riding in, and that campfire sure'n hell was theirs. Like as not they're setting around it eating . . . Saul, you take care of that lawdog. Want you to leave that judge to me and Devon. We got the right to kill him."

There was no comment from either Hillman or the younger Dixon, and then shortly Rye heard the quiet rustle of leaves as the men worked their way forward through the brush. Rye was at the edge of a small, open place just below the camp. A rainbird was calling into the night from somewhere in the distance, the sound lonely and forlorn, and in the dry leaves nearby a field mouse or some other small animal set up a rustling noise as it searched for food.

Abruptly the three men broke into view on the opposite side of the clearing. Little more than vague shadows, they were too indistinct to distinguish individual identities.

"Camp's right straight ahead—"

"Here's as close as you get!" Rye's voice was like the crack of a whip. "Dixon—you're all under arrest for interfering with the law! Throw down your guns and walk out into the middle of the clearing with your hands over your heads."

"The hell we will!" Gar Dixon shouted and, rocking to one side, triggered a shot at the lawman.

Rye, also moving, returned the fire. In that same moment, Devon Dixon and Saul Hillman opened up with their weapons. The lawman, throwing himself to the ground, fired three more quick shots at the shadows he could see. One yelled in pain and, staggering into the open, fell. Another toppled backward into the brush.

As smoke began to drift lazily into the clearing and the sharp smell of burnt gunpowder filled the air, Rye listened for sounds that would betray the location of the third man—Gar Dixon, he thought. He could hear nothing and, reloading his .45 and keeping low, he began to work his way through the brush in the direction the third man had taken. A sudden thought came to him. Gar Dixon was determined to put a bullet in Asa Metzgar; he could have made a run for the camp in hopes of getting a shot at the judge. Coming about, Rye hurriedly started to double back.

At that moment he heard the crackle of dry brush over to his left. Immediately the lawman veered and began to run toward the sound. After a few yards he halted and, smothering his gusty breathing as best he could, listened into the night. There was vague movement in the grove on ahead. Instantly Rye threw himself to one side.

The blast of a gun shattered the eerie stillness. Rye, catching a fleeting glimpse of Gar Dixon in the weak light, heard the thud of a bullet as it drove into the trunk of a nearby tree. He triggered his weapon instantly, aiming at the orange flare of Dixon's gun, only a short distance away. Gar returned the fire but the man apparently had no exact idea where the lawman was, as the bullet ripped through the undergrowth off to one side, missing its target even farther than the first.

Rye withheld further fire and, crouched, began to

move into the area between Dixon and the camp. There was more crackling, this time off to his left. He had placed himself between Dixon and the camp, he realized, which was what he wanted. Continuing to take advantage of the deep shadows, the marshal worked forward until he was behind a large tree. Rising, he faced into the direction he'd last heard movement from.

"Throw down your gun, Dixon!" he called. "Your son's dead. So is Hillman. Give it up!"

There was no reply. Rye, waiting out several minutes, began to move forward carefully. Dixon could be wounded, having been hit by one of the lawman's earlier shots, or he could have been cut down by one of the bullets in the exchange that had just taken place. He pushed on slowly and as silently as possible, listening for the swish of branches swinging back into place, the crackle of a dry twig, or the rustle of leaves.

The lawman halted as the quick pound of a running horse going north brought him up short. Dixon had pulled out. Rye swore feelingly. He had wanted to settle with the man and his party one way or another, here and now. Instead Dixon was running out and, worst of all, would be ahead of them where he could wait in ambush. The lawman shook his head wearily. Nothing seemed to pan out, he thought. He'd had nothing but trouble since leaving Arizona with Hanging Judge Metzgar in his custody.

Turning, he started back to camp. He'd get Metzgar and together they would recover Hillman and Devon Dixon's horses, lead them to where the two men lay and load up the bodies. Then he would decide whether to bury them along the trail or, if they weren't too far from a settlement, to take them on and turn them over to the town's lawman for proper burial.

A few miles down the river Jake Bedford was squatting by a low fire, drinking a cup of coffee, when the distant rattle of gunshots reached him. He did not look up; there was no point as the shooting was somewhere on to the north and certainly beyond the reach of his vision.

Setting the empty cup aside, he began to unwrap the bandage on his arm. It was time to apply some of the medicine the doctor in Taos had given him.

"You're going to lose that arm if you ain't careful," the physician had warned. "It's mighty close to mortifying now. Why the devil didn't you come see me before this?"

"Wasn't anywheres close by," Bedford had said. "You just fix it up best you can and give me medicine to take along."

"You planning on going somewhere?"

"Somewhere," Bedford had replied. "Don't exactly know where, but I ain't stopping till I get there."

The doctor, a small, thin man wearing a dusty blue suit and pince-nez glasses, had frowned. "You're not making sense, but I reckon you know what you're doing."

Jake had nodded. Then, "What's the quickest way to get to Nebraska?"

"Nebraska! Mister, you're on the wrong side of the mountains. You ought to be on the old Santa Fe Trail Cutoff. It'll take you up to Kansas—"

"Said Nebraska."

"Wait'll I've finished, dammit! You get to Kansas,

then ride north, that's how you get to Nebraska. How'd you happen to wind up here?"

"Took the wrong trail out of Santa Fe. There a road that'll take me through the mountains and put me on the right track?"

"Yes, sure is. Double back the way you come till you come to a fork. Take the left-hand one. It'll take you to a town called Cimarron. A ways east of it you can get on the main Santa Fe Trail, but if you want what they call the Cimarron Cutoff, which will be shorter to Kansas, you'll have to keep on going east."

Jake had thanked the physician, paid his two-dollar fee, which included not only the tending and dressing of the wound but a small can of disinfecting salve as well, and ridden on. Days later, at a place called McNees Crossing, he traded his jaded horse for one in better condition, after which he pressed on at a faster pace.

From a sutler who'd set up his wagon a short distance inside the Kansas line, he learned that a party of two men and a woman had passed that way headed for Nebraska. The descriptions fit Metzgar and the lawman; the woman was probably some doxy one of them had brought along for cold nights. Important thing—he was now on the right trail and, restocking his grub sack from the trader's wagon, Jake hurried on.

He reached the Republican River late one afternoon under a cloudy sky and made camp. Both he and the horse were worn out, and as he stirred up a meal of salt pork and chunked potatoes he wondered how much farther it would be to Nebraska, and just how far behind Metzgar and the lawman he was.

Not too far, he was certain. He had pressed his horse

hard, building the big gelding up each night with a large ration of grain so that he could take the coming day's work without faltering.

If at all possible he wanted to overtake Metzgar and the lawman—and now a woman—before they reached whatever destination in Nebraska they had in mind. He couldn't seem to recall if the name of the town Metzgar was going to had been mentioned back in Hudkins' saloon or not. It didn't matter a damn, Bedford had long since decided; he'd follow Metzgar —the hanging judge who had murdered his brother— till hell froze over, if need be.

22

It began to rain shortly after midnight. Rye, maintaining a watch over the camp in the event Gar Dixon made another attempt to kill Asa Metzgar, had anticipated the change of weather. Hunched, back to a tree, long slicker pulled about him, he was finding the minutes not too uncomfortable.

He had no idea just what to expect from Dixon. The man was a loony—half crazed with hate for Metzgar—but it seemed unlikely to the lawman that a father would forsake the body of his son, although it could be possible, he supposed, where that of Saul Hillman, a lesser relative, was concerned.

The sky had cleared by morning, leaving the land sparkling green and freshly washed. As soon as it was light, Rye walked to a nearby knoll and searched the country ahead with his glass, looking for signs of Dixon. The effort failed and, disturbed, he returned to camp.

Both Moriah and Asa were up, the woman, as was usual, going about the business of getting a meal ready. No fire had as yet been built, the judge seemingly content to leave that chore to Rye while he attended the horses; or it could have been he was at a loss as to where he could find dry wood after so wet a night. The lawman had no difficulty; working in under the thick branches of the trees, close to the trunk, he managed to collect a good armload of dry fuel. In a short time he had a fire going for Moriah to cook by as well as another to drive the chill from their bones.

But there was a pall hanging over the camp as a result of the shoot-out with the Dixons. And while John Rye had long since adjusted his conscience and way of life to such incidents, and Asa Metzgar did not appear affected to any extent, Rye could see that Moriah Tuttle was struggling to control her feelings. Several times he caught her staring at the blanket- and canvas-wrapped bodies of Devon Dixon and Saul Hillman hung across their saddles and had wondered earlier if, for her sake, he might better have buried them back at the clearing instead of electing to take them on into the next settlement. Finally, an hour or so after they had gotten under way, she rode in beside him.

"Marshal—I'm curious. Do you enjoy your job?" she asked.

The lawman considered her for a long minute, fully aware of the meaning underlying her words. "If you mean using my gun on a man, the answer is no."

"But you shot and killed two men last night. Doesn't that affect you—do something to you?"

"Maybe not in the way you're thinking. They were men out to break the law—to kill. I had no choice but to stop them."

"They weren't really outlaws—"

"The way I see it they were. I tried to talk them out of what they intended to do—kill the judge—a long way back, but they wouldn't listen to me. Just wanted revenge."

"Vengeance can be a terribly bitter thing," the woman murmured, shaking her head.

"Like the marshal said, he didn't have a choice," Metzgar said, coming into the conversation as the horses plodded steadily on over the rain-softened plain. "His job is to keep me alive, and that's what he was doing."

Rye glanced about. He had purposely struck a course well out in the open, one a good half mile from any brush and trees, thus avoiding, as much as possible, a place where Gar Dixon could set up an ambush.

"Can't say I've cared much for the job," the lawman said, blunt as always.

"No grounds that I can see for you being so damn choosy," Metzgar shot back. "Like I've mentioned, I don't see a lot of difference in you and me. I send men to their deaths for committing a crime. You kill them before they do. Proves out about the same."

Rye was silent for a long breath, his pale eyes on a hawk winging its way effortlessly toward the west.

"They have a choice with me," he said. "Nothing says they have to shoot it out. They can come along peaceably."

"And then have to face a judge," Moriah said. "Seems to me they don't have any choice at all."

"They had a choice in the first place: they didn't have to become outlaws." Rye's voice was stiff. He didn't like the subject and wished the woman would drop it.

"Perhaps," she said. "Sometimes circumstances dictate what—"

"Plenty of other men are faced with hardship and bad luck, and whatever you mean by circumstances, and don't turn to being an outlaw. Taking up a gun is the easy way out."

"I'm not sure I agree, but—"

"You'd not see it the marshal's way," Metzgar said. "Being a woman you've got a kind heart—a soft heart.

You don't want to see anything hurt, and you're filled with trust. Believe me, Moriah, a man can't look at it your way. If he did, this country would be overrun by outlaws. You agree, Marshal?"

Rye nodded. He didn't particularly agree with Asa Metzgar on anything, but in that he was in full accord: the country had to have laws, and laws had to be enforced.

"Expect you're right—"

Rye looked ahead. The land was changing. The long, slightly rolling flat over which they were crossing was now beginning to slope downward and appeared to break off into an area of low hills and bluffs. He swung his attention to the east, not liking the idea of passing through ragged country that would afford many opportunities for Gar Dixon to lie in wait for them. It would take a bit longer to reach Nebraska and the town where Asa Metzgar lived, but getting the man there alive was the important thing even if—

A rider burst suddenly from the shadow of a bluff at the edge of the plain. Rye hauled back on the chestnut's reins, bringing him to a quick halt.

"It's Dixon!" he shouted at Metzgar and the woman. "Get off your horses—and stay low!"

At once he raked the gelding with his spurs, sent him rushing forward to intercept the charging Dixon. In the next moment Gar, hunched low in his saddle, opened up with his gun. Rye, his weapon out, snapped a hurried shot at the man. Dixon flinched but came on at full gallop, shooting as he did, the bullets directed not at the lawman but at the crouching Asa Metzgar.

Gar Dixon had lost his senses completely. Hate and the death of another son, which he undoubtedly blamed on the judge, too, had thoroughly deranged the man's mind, and he was now out to kill Metzgar at any cost.

Rye triggered another bullet at Dixon and cut sharply away. He was hoping to just wound the man, with the thought that the shock might bring Gar to his senses. It was a lost hope. Dixon, ignoring the lawman, raced on toward Metzgar and Moriah Tuttle, both now lying flat on the ground. Beyond them Metzgar's bay was pitching wildly, squealing with every jump. Evidently one of Dixon's bullets had struck him. Nearby the packhorse was shying nervously. The little bay appeared unhurt but was frightened by the actions of Metzgar's animal.

Rye, grim-faced, eyes on Dixon, could wait no longer. In a few more moments Gar would be close enough to where one of his bullets could not miss Metzgar. Raising his gun, he lowered it until it was leveled at Dixon and pressed off a shot. Gar immediately straightened up in his saddle. His horse slowed, began to curve off to one side. Suddenly Dixon buckled forward and fell to the ground.

Rye, face taut, rode through the faint smoke haze hanging about him, on to where Dixon lay. Pulling up, he dismounted, knelt briefly beside the man and felt for signs of life. Gar was dead. Coming upright, he reloaded his weapon, slid it back into the holster and, features still a rocklike mask, crossed to where Dixon's horse had stopped and, taking up the reins, led it back to where its rider lay.

"You got him!" Metzgar said in a triumphant sort of voice as he and the woman, leading their mounts, hurried up. "Thought for a bit there I was a goner. Why did you take so long to bring him down?"

Rye, busy removing the blanket roll from Dixon's

horse, did not reply. Maybe he did cut it a bit close before he triggered the bullet that killed Gar Dixon. He had hoped to the last that it wouldn't be necessary —but it had gone for nothing.

"Give me a hand here," he said. He had unrolled the blanket and tarp and laid them out flat.

Metzgar stepped up to the lifeless body and, taking it by the heels while Rye lifted the shoulders, they together placed Dixon on the square of fabric and rolled him into it. That done, Rye tied the tarp and woolen cover securely at both ends to prevent its coming loose, after which the two men hung the body across the gray's saddle.

"That man was sure out to kill me," Metzgar said as the marshal anchored the body to the saddle. "Was a lunatic, a pure, out-and-out lunatic."

"He'd had his three sons killed," Rye said quietly. "Reckon that's enough to send any man over the edge."

"You're not forgetting they were outlaws, are you?"

"The two you hung, I guess. But the one called Devon was only doing what his pa told him to. Hardly call him an outlaw."

"When he and his pa came after me with guns all set to shoot me down, I figure that makes them outlaws, too . . . You want to look at my horse? One of Dixon's bullets grazed him."

Rye crossed to Asa's bay. There was a bloody streak across the gelding's hindquarters. The bullet had only grooved his hide, causing no serious wound.

"One hit the pack saddle, too," Moriah said. "Probably put holes in some of the pans."

"Lucky," Rye said laconically and, turning back to where Gar Dixon's horse was patiently waiting, led the animal to the end of the string and attached his lead rope to the saddle of the last horse in line. They'd make a hell of a procession riding into Metzgar's home town, he thought. Three dead men hung across their saddles; his reputation as a killer marshal would grow considerably now. No one would bother to learn the facts, they'd simply draw their own conclusions and credit him with shooting down three men.

Mounting up, he started to move out, aware in that moment that Moriah Tuttle had ridden up and was alongside him.

"Marshal, I just wanted you to know that I saw what you did—"

"Meaning what?" he demanded gruffly as they started forward.

"That you held back from shooting that man. I think you were trying to make him stop."

Rye shrugged. "Reckon that doesn't matter much now," the lawman said. "He's dead."

23

They reached the town of Plattesville, lying on a rise adjacent to the river from which it had taken its name, late one morning. Somnolent, sun-baked, it looked little different from a hundred other such towns to John Rye, but to Asa Metzgar it immediately took on the aspect of a queen city.

"That's the hotel, there on the corner. Looks just about the same as it did when I left," he said, pointing. "And there's the church where I went to Sunday school. Hasn't changed much either. Looks like we've got a couple more saloons, and a livery stable."

Metzgar rattled on, taking much pride in naming the various buildings to Moriah as they continued along the single main street paralleling the river. Rye was paying little mind to the jurist's words, his interest lying in locating the Plattesville jail and marshal's office where he could discharge his responsibilities.

There were, at first, only three or four persons on the street, but their number had grown as the grim little cavalcade moved toward the center of the town. The lawman, in the lead and trailing the string of three horses carrying canvas-wrapped bodies, looked neither to the right nor to the left. Metzgar and Moriah Tuttle were off to his right while the packhorse, his customary place immediately behind Rye's chestnut usurped by the lead horse in the string, now walked beside the lawman.

"What's going on?" he heard a man ask. "Who are they?"

At that moment the marshal spotted the jail. It was on the opposite corner from the hotel. Evidently small in size, it bore the sign "Town Marshal" above its door.

"We'll leave you here," Metzgar called when they drew near the hostelry. "Aim to get a room for myself and one for Moriah so's we—"

"That'll have to wait. My job's not done till I turn you over to the law here," Rye said, and angled toward the jail.

Coming to the hitch rack, he sighed gratefully and swung off the chestnut. Looping the reins around the crossbar, he turned to the three horses strung out into the street, drew them in and methodically, one by one, tied them to the bar alongside the chestnut.

"Who you got rolled up in them tarps, mister?" a man in the thickening crowd called.

Rye shook his head in reply and glanced up at Asa Metzgar, still in the saddle. "Climb down. Want the marshal to know who you are. The lady can go on to the hotel."

Metzgar frowned irritably, nodded to the woman. "Go ahead, sign in for our rooms. I won't be long."

"You a lawman of some kind?"

"Bounty hunter more'n likely—bringing in three dead men like he is," a hostile voice commented.

Rye continued to ignore the crowd and, waiting until Metzgar was at his side, stepped up onto the weathered board landing fronting the jail and entered. There was no one in the small, cramped office.

"Hell—I know who that big jasper is!" someone said from the street. "That's Rye—the one they call the Doomsday Marshal."

"Killer marshal, you mean. Hear tell he never brings a man in alive; easier to do it with them hanging across their saddle."

Rye listened indifferently as Metzgar sank onto one of the benches placed against the wall. He'd learned long ago that a man seldom got credit for the good things he did, invariably became noted for the bad things people thought he did.

Walking to the door, the lawman looked out over the crowd gathered before the building. "Where the hell's the marshal?" he said to no one in particular and then turned back.

He had finished the job assigned him, needed only to hand Asa Metzgar over to the town's lawman, and the disagreeable chore would be over. After that he could get on with the rest of the business he had with the marshal: the bodies of Saul Hillman and the Dixons.

"I'm not waiting any longer," Metzgar declared, coming to his feet. "The marshal could be out of town, not be back for days. You bother to ask anybody about him? No, you're too damn stiff-backed to—"

"You men looking for me?" a voice asked from the doorway. "I'm Hays, the town marshal."

Rye nodded, reached into the inner pocket of his fringed coat and produced the wallet containing his official identity and presidential authority papers, and handed them to the lawman. He waited while Hays, a tall, sandy-looking man somewhere in his thirties, read the documents.

"Guess what I heard out there in the street's right," he said, returning the folder to Rye. "This got something to do with those dead men you brought in?"

"Partly . . . Man here with me is Judge Asa Metzgar—"

"I used to live here," the jurist cut in. "Got some farmland right outside town. Maybe you remember me."

Hays pursed his lips, brushed at his mustache and shook his head. "No, can't say as I do. Must've been a long time ago."

"It was," Rye said. "The judge has been away for a good many years. Made himself quite a few enemies during that time; three of them are out there slung across their saddles."

"Why did you—"

"He resigned being a judge," Rye said, anticipating the question, "and the law ordered me to see that he got home safe. Still a few around who'd like to even a score with him."

"Only natural," Metzgar said with a shrug. "I did what was my sworn duty. Calling me what they do is unfair."

Hays was still having trouble understanding. "What do you mean? Call you what?"

"A hanging judge," Rye said when Metzgar made no reply. "I got him here alive, up to you now to see he stays that way."

"Hell, I can't take on no job like that!" Hays protested. "I don't even have a deputy."

"Oh, you won't have any problems there, Marshal," Metzgar said hurriedly. "Nobody knows me around here. Served my time as judge in Texas, Arizona Territory and the country around them."

"A man can get from there to here by riding, same as you did," Hays said in a falling voice. "I'll do the best I can, Rye . . . Now, what about those dead men out there?" he added, jerking a thumb toward the hitch rack. The crowd gathered before the jail had grown larger, and there was a steady rumble of conversation.

"If you don't need me any longer I'll go on to the hotel," Metzgar said, moving toward the door.

Hays glanced at Rye, who nodded. "All right," the younger lawman said. "We can get together later on, hash out what's the best thing for us to do." He fell silent then as the judge left, but after a moment added: "What's his big hurry? He don't look any more wore out from riding than you do."

Rye smiled, took out his cigar case. Offering one of the slim black stogies to Hays, who declined, he selected one for himself.

"Was a woman joined up with us back in New Mexico," he explained. "Had to get to some town over near Scottsbluff in a hurry; sick mother, I think she said. Didn't have much choice but to take her along. She's over at the hotel now."

"Guess the judge got kind of sweet on her—"

"Did for a fact. Were talking marriage. The judge has a farm around here somewhere. Intends to settle down and start farming."

"He really got the reputation of being a hanging judge?"

Rye struck a match to his stogie and puffed it into life. "He has. Those dead men out there you were asking about followed him all the way from Arizona looking for the chance to kill him."

"But ended up dead themselves. Your gun?"

"My gun," Rye said, stepping to the door and flipping the used match into the dirt. He glanced coldly, appraisingly, at the crowd. It fell silent at his appearance. Indifferent, he turned back to the lawman.

"Did all I could to avoid a shoot-out but they wouldn't have it any other way. Be obliged if you'll see they get a decent burial. Two of them's named Dixon, other is Hillman."

"Sure. What about their belongings?"

"Ship whatever there is to the sheriff in Prescott, Arizona. Can sell off their horses and gear to pay for the burying and any other charges."

Hays nodded and, moving past John Rye, stepped out onto the landing. Glancing about, he pointed to a man in the forefront of the crowd.

"Jensen, take them dead men over to the undertaker's and then stable their horses. Can tell Blakemore or whoever's at the livery barn that I'll be over after a while."

"What about Swinford? First thing he'll ask is who's going to pay for burying the stiffs," Jensen said, starting to collect the horses' lead ropes.

"Tell him the same thing . . . Now, the rest of you folks, move on. Ain't nothing here that's any of your business," Hays said and swung back into his office.

"Can expect another fellow with the same idea those three had to show up," Rye said, relaxing on one of the benches. "Lost him back near Santa Fe, but I don't think he's the kind that will give up."

"Same thing—shoot the Hanging Judge—that it?"

Rye smiled. "The same. Calls himself Jake Bedford. Judge hung his brother. Bedford claims there was no need."

"Never is if you listen to the relatives of the outlaws that got strung up. You staying over?"

"Aim to. Haven't had a good night's sleep since I left Arizona," Rye said, coming to his feet, and crossed to the doorway. A tight smile parted his lips. The crowd was still there. Again Hays pushed by him.

"Told you all to break it up. I mean it!"

"We're wanting to know what that killer marshal's going to do," a man near the front of the gathering yelled.

"We don't want him around here. This is our town and—"

The speaker broke off as two muffled gunshots sounded along the street. Immediately Hays hurried out onto the landing. "Where'd those shots come from?"

"The hotel," someone in the crowd answered and, as one, the entire gathering shifted and began to move for the structure on the opposite corner.

Rye, a frown pulling at his brow, followed Hays off the landing and started for the hotel. Had Jake Bedford somehow gotten ahead of him and, awaiting an opportunity, settled his score? Or was it another enemy of Asa Metzgar's who came upon him unexpectedly and seized the moment to satisfy his craving for vengeance?

"Probably a couple of damn drunks shooting it out in the hotel's bar," Rye heard Hays say in a low, angry voice as they hurried along the dusty street.

Rye nodded grimly. He only hoped it was the truth.

24

The two lawmen reached the corner of the hotel, mounted the steps leading up onto the porch and with the noisy crowd piling up in the street behind them ran toward the door. At that moment the screened framework flung open and a man rushed into the open.

"Somebody get Doc Davis!" he yelled. "A man's been shot!"

"Who is it, Charlie?" Hays asked as the man wheeled back to the entrance.

"Don't know. Stranger," Charlie replied. "You better get in here, too, Marshal."

Stranger. It would have to be Metzgar, Rye thought and, crowding past Hays, followed Charlie into the lobby of the hotel. Hand resting on the butt of his gun, the lawman allowed his eyes to adjust to the sudden change of light and glanced around.

A half dozen men were clustered at the foot of the stairs leading up to the second floor. Rye, crossing quickly to them, followed their upward gaze. Sprawled at the top, one arm dangling over onto the step, was Asa Metzgar. The upper part of his body and shoulder appeared to be covered with blood—and standing just beyond him, gun in hand, was Moriah Tuttle.

"My God—some woman's gone and shot the judge,"

Hays, at Rye's side, muttered. "Ain't she the one that rode in with you?"

"She is," Rye answered and, eyes on the woman, began to slowly mount the stairs. Smoke still hung in the motionless air around her and a strong, acrid odor was spreading through the area.

"Watch out!" one of the men standing in the lobby warned. "She'll shoot you, too—sure'n hell! Shot that fellow once in her room, then when he come staggering out through the door, she shot him again."

Rye continued to climb the stairs. He was wondering what prompted the woman to kill, or try to kill, Metzgar. They had become very close, he thought—had even talked about marriage. What had happened?

Midway up the staircase Rye saw Moriah's eyes shift from Metzgar's crumpled shape to him. He shook his head.

"Stand easy, Mrs. Tuttle. Everything's going to be all right," he said quietly.

A bit of the tautness seemed to leave Moriah's tense body. Her arms relaxed at her sides. Rye finished climbing the stairs, carefully stepping over Metzgar, and halted before her.

"Best you give me that gun," he said and, reaching out, took the weapon from her. Down below there was a quick burst of conversation as a young man in shirtsleeves, carrying a satchel, entered and hurried up the stairs. Following him closely were Marshal Hays and two other men. Rye, taking Moriah by the arm, gently guided her back through the open doorway of the room nearby, one evidently hers.

"Help me get him up off the step and laying flat," Rye heard the physician say. "Can't treat him where he is, all sprawled out like he is."

Moriah looked directly at Rye. "Is he dead?"

The lawman shook his head. "Don't know. Won't till the doctor gets through . . . Why'd you shoot him, Mrs. Tuttle? I thought you two were close—more than friends."

"Friends!" she echoed. "I hated him! Have ever since the day he hung my husband back in Arkansas."

Rye stared at her. "You were in Las Vegas—in New Mexico when—"

"That's where I went to build a new life and forget the past. I'd almost forgotten about Arkansas when I heard Judge Metzgar was in town. I guess all the hate backed up in me sort of broke loose at hearing his name."

"And you got us to let you come along, saying you had to go to your mother, so you could kill him."

"Yes, that—that was all a lie. I'm sorry I deceived you, Marshal; you're a decent man. But I had to have a reason."

"I think he'll be all right. Bullets went too high to hit any vital organs . . . Did break a couple of bones."

Rye listened to the doctor's words. Relieved, he came back to Moriah. "Knowing now how you feel, I'm surprised you waited until we got here before you used your gun. Some reason?"

Moriah was looking through the doorway at the cluster of men beyond. "He's still alive, isn't he?"

"So far . . . Why didn't you shoot him sometime back on the trail?" the marshal asked, repeating himself.

"That's what I intended to do, but you were always around and I never really got the chance. There were a couple of times when I could have, but I didn't have my pistol with me. Finally gave up trying, just decided to wait until we got here."

"Even though you know you'd be caught and charged with murder? On the trail you maybe could have gotten away with it."

"I know, but I didn't expect to get away with it. I just didn't care . . . I—I hope—now—that he doesn't die."

"Good chance he won't," Rye said and, stepping to the doorway, beckoned to Hays.

"I don't know what you want to do with this lady, Marshal," he said. "Looks like the judge is going to make it, and she's sorry now that she shot him." Rye paused, glanced at Moriah. "Can chalk it up as a sort of lovers' quarrel. Think you can let her go on her way?"

"Sort of figured it was a spat between lovers," Hays said, nodding. "Well, long as the judge ain't dead and ain't likely to die according to the doc, I don't see why not. Might be smart, however, if she'd catch the next stage out of town."

Rye turned to Moriah. "That agreeable to you?"

The woman nodded woodenly and then glanced at Rye. Her eyes expressed her thanks. "Yes, I'll go—no matter where."

"Goes to Scottsbluff," Hays said. "I'll see that they have a seat for you."

Rye came about and, smiling at Moriah Tuttle, moved toward the stairs. The doctor was still working over Asa Metzgar, wrapping bandages about his chest and shoulder. The lawman did not stop but, reaching the top of the stairway, descended slowly, weariness finally having its way with him. He'd thought of spending the night in Plattesville, but the idea no longer appealed to him. He'd feel better on the trail; a hotel bed could wait a few more days.

Passing through the two dozen or so men gathered in the lobby, who made way in sullen silence as he approached, Rye stepped out onto the porch. A curse slipped past his hard-set mouth. A brightness came into his eyes. In the act of dismounting at the hotel's hitch rack was Jake Bedford.

Bedford saw Rye at almost the same instant. He came about, hands dropping to his sides. The remnants of the crowd in the street pulled back, sensing trouble.

"Where is he?" Bedford demanded in a hard voice.

"You're too late," the lawman replied and, skirting the truth, added, "He's already been shot."

Bedford swore deeply. "You cheated me out of what I had coming, lawman, and I ain't letting you get away with it!"

"Was doing my job. Forget it."

"No, I ain't about to! Aim to take my satisfaction out on you; I've still got one good arm."

Rye studied the rancher coldly. Bedford, dusty, face covered with whiskers, eyes bloodshot from the long days on the trail and sagging with fatigue, was in no condition to do anything but rest.

"I'll say it again, Bedford, forget it. Go on back home. You've got no quarrel with me."

"The hell I—"

"Reach for that gun you're carrying and I'll have to kill you—and there's been enough of that," Rye said coldly. The crowd, standing back at a safe distance, was silent, taking in every word of the confrontation.

"I ain't backing off!" Bedford yelled and made a stab for his gun.

Before the rancher's weapon had completely cleared its holster, the lawman's gun was out and leveled—but John Rye did not fire.

"Warned you, Bedford: you wouldn't have a chance," the marshal said in a low, frustrated voice. "All I have to do is pull the trigger and you're dead; but I won't."

A sudden burst of conversations arose in the crowd. Rye glanced toward the gathering. A derisive smile parted his lips.

"Leave that gun where it is, Jake, and you'll stay alive," he said.

Pivoting on a heel, he holstered his weapon and walked stiffly on to where his horses waited in front of the Plattesburg jail. Mounting the chestnut, he cut about and, with the bay packhorse following, struck a course east. There'd been no new orders waiting for him; he guessed he was free to do as he wished—at least for a while. Dodge City would be a good place to go. He'd like to hunt up John Smith and Shorty Pedgett, if that's where they had been bound for, and see just who the hell they were.